'And how long are you going to keep this up?'

Rose gulped nervously. 'Keep what up?'

'Pretending that last night didn't happen.'

'I suppose I just wasn't ready for it,' she mumbled. 'It was too soon. I wasn't expecting it.'

There was no amusement in his slate-grey eyes now. 'I think that you've been expecting it ever since the day you moved in here,' Nathan told her softly.

'How can you say that?' she said with sudden fierceness. 'Soon after I came here, you told me that you weren't interested in me, that I wasn't your type. Then I had to hear all about your obsession with Jancis Kendall, and how *she* was the only one you always wanted in your bed. How was I to know you'd take me for a substitute, since she wasn't around any longer?'

Books you will enjoy
by JOANNA MANSELL

THE SEDUCTION OF SARA

Sara was certain Lucas Farraday was just a penniless drifter, and she wasn't too pleased when he kept following her on her exhausting trip around Peru. But gradually she began to relax and get used to his presence and his help—and that was when he made his next move...

DEVIL IN PARADISE

When Kate inherited a half-share in a villa in the South of France, she headed straight out there for the summer—to find Rafe Clarendon, her co-heir, already installed. Kate had enough problems getting through the door—she had no idea how much trouble was to follow...

A KISS BY CANDLELIGHT

Cathryn wasn't quite sure how she'd let her boss talk her into looking after his injured brother for two weeks—she was a secretary, not a nursemaid! Sir Charles had warned her that Nicholas was a bad-tempered bully—but he'd forgotten to add that he was also very attractive...

EGYPTIAN NIGHTS

Ellie had been through a bad time, but now, as part of her new job, she was accompanying a group of schoolgirls and their deputy headmistress on a trip to Egypt, and things seemed to be improving. Until Leo Copeland arrived on the scene, and put Ellie in a most compromising situation!

HAUNTED SUMMER

BY

JOANNA MANSELL

MILLS & BOON LIMITED
ETON HOUSE   18-24 PARADISE ROAD
RICHMOND   SURREY   TW9 1SR

First published in Great Britain 1990
by Mills & Boon Limited

© Joanna Mansell 1990

Australian copyright 1990
Philippine copyright 1990
This edition 1990

ISBN 0 263 76816 3

Set in Times Roman 10½ on 12 pt.
01-9009-52800 C

Made and printed in Great Britain

CHAPTER ONE

ROSE pulled the car over to the side of the deserted country lane, studied the map spread out on the seat beside her, and then gave a deep sigh.

'I think I'm lost,' she muttered gloomily.

She peered out of the car window, and then gave another sigh. There wasn't even any sign of a house. Just trees, fields, birds and blue sky, as the road wound its way into a sunlit wooded valley.

Rose found it hard to believe that she was only a few miles from the small but bustling seaside town on the North Devon coast, where she was staying. She felt as if she were in the middle of nowhere.

'Oh, well, I suppose I'd better keep going,' she finally decided. Then she gave a small grimace. She didn't actually have much choice. The lane was too narrow for her to turn the car round and go back the way she had come.

She drove on cautiously, keeping her speed well down in case she suddenly met something coming from the other direction. Not that that seemed very likely! She hadn't seen another car since she had turned on to this road.

The sides of the valley became steeper, trapping the sunshine, which blazed hotly through the car windows. Rose ran her fingers through her mop of golden-brown hair, and wished she were sitting on the beach with a cooling breeze blowing off the sea. She could

have left this trip until tomorrow, and spent today
making the most of this sudden blaze of fine weather.

Only, if she had done that, it might have jeopard-
ised her chances of getting the job she was going for.
Someone else could easily have got there before her.
And she really needed to find work. She was beginning to run embarrassingly short of money.

A faded signpost caught her attention, and she
brought the car to a halt. 'Lyncombe Manor' it said
in rather uneven lettering, and Rose gave a grin of
pure relief. She had found it! The instructions she had
been given in the small shop, where she had seen the
card giving details of the job, hadn't been completely
useless after all.

She drove on with fresh enthusiasm, the car
windows wound down to let in the warm, sweet-
scented air. There was one last sharp bend in the lane,
and then it curved gently round to a house that Rose
knew had to be Lyncombe Manor.

She stopped the car and just gazed at the house
with wide eyes. It was beautiful! Whitewashed walls,
lattice windows set in a jumble of gables, tall chim-
neys, a slate roof patterned with lichen, and a riot of
roses that sprawled over just about everything,
throwing up great sprays of blooms and showering
the gravel drive with drifts of fallen petals, white, pink,
red, yellow, and a dozen shades in between.

Rose parked the car a little way from the house;
then she got out and slowly began to walk towards it.
She wanted to approach it on foot so she could take
in the details more thoroughly, letting her eyes feast
on the picturesque old house in its idyllic setting.

The front door and all the windows were closed,
and she had the impression that no one was at home.

She didn't mind that, though. It would give her a chance to look around before the owner returned.

There was an open archway at the side of the house, and Rose couldn't resist going through it. It led into the grounds at the back of the house, which were wildly overgrown. The card in the shop had advertised for a gardener, and Rose decided that they definitely needed one! Whether they would consider her suitable was something that she still had to find out. She knew a lot about plants, and she was strong and healthy, but she knew that the fact that she was female might prove the sticking-point, especially if the owners of Lyncombe Manor were rather old-fashioned.

She wandered a little further into the garden. On the left was a sunken area with a large pond, where a lot of ducks paddled happily around, and other water birds were pottering in and out of the rushes at the far end. The main area of lawn obviously hadn't been cut for ages and looked more like a meadow, while the flower-beds which ranged down both sides were smothered with weeds, although a surprising number of flowers were managing to push their way through and send up bright splashes of bloom. Half a dozen great trees, including a magnificent copper beech, provided welcome patches of shade, and Rose could picture how the garden would look when it was cleared and restored to its former glory. In fact, her fingers itched to make a start on it.

'First things first,' she reminded herself drily. 'You haven't even got the job yet!'

She wondered how long she would have to wait for someone to come back to the house. Perhaps they had just gone out for a couple of hours, and would

be returning fairly soon. She didn't really mind if they
weren't back until much later, though. She was perfectly happy to roam around in the hot sunshine, enjoying the peace and tranquillity of this place.

She glanced at her watch and was surprised to find
that it was already fairly late in the afternoon. She
hadn't realised it had taken her so long to get here.
It didn't matter, though. In fact, it meant that the
owners would probably be back sooner than she had
expected. With luck, they were already heading back
home for tea.

Rose thought that they probably wouldn't mind if
she took a closer look at the house while she was
waiting for them to return. She strolled towards the
back of Lyncombe Manor, and found that it was built
around a small cobbled courtyard. Like the rest of
the house, it was an enchanting place, splashed with
sunshine, yet with shady corners where tubs of ferns
flourished in the cooler conditions.

She peered through one of the windows, feeling a
little guilty about being so blatantly nosy, but itching
to know what the house looked like inside. The sun
was reflecting off the glass, though, and she couldn't
see anything very clearly. She backed away again and
decided to sit for a while on the seat on the far side
of the courtyard. She supposed it was a bit of a cheek,
making herself at home like this, but people in this
part of the world were always very welcoming and
friendly. She didn't think the owners of the house
would object at all if she just sat there in the sun for
half an hour.

Rose closed her eyes blissfully as the late afternoon
sunshine beat down on her face. That meant she didn't
see the door open on the far side of the courtyard.

Nor did she see the man who stood there for several long seconds, staring at her. And because he moved absolutely silently, she didn't hear him walk over to her.

The first she knew of his presence was when a hard hand clamped over her shoulder, making her yelp out loud in startled surprise. Her eyes flew open, and as her head shot up she found herself staring at a man who was clearly in the grip of a cold, intense anger.

'On your feet!' he ordered curtly.

Rose was so stunned by this violent end to the quiet peacefulness of the afternoon that she immediately obeyed. As soon as she was standing up, he whipped her round and began to march her forcibly towards the open doorway.

'Hey!' she said sharply, finally managing to find her voice. 'What are you doing?'

'You wanted to see inside the house?' the man said grimly. 'Well, you won't have to peer through the windows any more. I'm going to let you see it at much closer quarters.'

'I know that was very rude of me, and I do apologise——' Rose began, her voice quite breathless now because they were moving at some speed.

'I'm not interested in apologies,' he cut in shortly. 'But I *am* interested in teaching people like you a lesson that you won't quickly forget.'

They were through the doorway now, and Rose found herself being frogmarched through the kitchen and then along a narrow passage with a stone-flagged floor.

'People like me?' she echoed, beginning to feel pretty panic-stricken now. Who *was* this man—and what did he intend to do with her?

'You're parasites,' he growled, his voice laced with pure contempt. 'Living off other people's lives, forcing your way into private houses, never damned well giving up——' They were halfway along the passage-way now, and he abruptly stopped and opened a door on his right. 'You were determined to get in here somehow, weren't you?' he challenged her, his eyes alight again with that anger that was all the more frightening because of its coldness. 'Well, you've made it. In fact, I'm even inviting you to stay for a while.'

He released that painful grip on her shoulder. Before she had time to feel relieved that he had finally let go of her, he gave her a hard shove which sent her staggering through the doorway. There was a flight of stairs just inside, and Rose lost her balance and half tumbled down them. Bruised and shocked, she dragged herself back to her feet. Then she stared up at him as he lounged in the doorway, looking at her with an impersonal satisfaction that completely chilled her blood.

'Are you totally crazy?' she somehow got out in a voice that was audibly shaking now.

'No, not crazy,' he replied tightly. 'Just sick to death of intrusions into my private life. I don't know how you found me, but since you're here you're going to be given a privilege that I hope you'll appreciate. You're the first—and the last—reporter who will ever set foot inside this house.'

'I'm not a reporter!' Rose denied frantically, but it was too late. He had already slammed the door shut.

Panic really began to set in after that. She scrambled up the steps and began hammering on the thick door, at the same time shouting at the top of her voice. She yelled at him to let her out, she threatened to sue him if he kept her locked in here, and finally ended up begging him to open it, but nothing worked. The door remained shut.

Trembling with exertion and shock, Rose slowly drew back from the door and huddled in a small ball on the top step.

'I don't believe this is happening,' she muttered in a quavering voice. 'I don't believe *any* of this is really happening.'

But the cold stone step beneath her was real enough. And so was the closed and locked door.

Shivering a little now with reaction, she lifted her head and slowly looked around. She guessed she was in some kind of cellar. It was lit by a single dim light bulb, and there seemed to be a lot of rubbish piled in one corner, as if someone had been having a clear-out and dumped most of the stuff down here.

Goose-pimples ran over her skin again, and Rose realised it wasn't just from the shock of what had happened. It was quite cold down here. It was hard to believe there was warm sunshine still blazing down outside the house.

After what seemed like a very long time, she finally felt strong enough to stand up. Her legs still felt fairly shaky, but she was beginning to feel very angry now, as well as scared. She had already worked out what had happened. That man had obviously thought she was a reporter snooping around—and he clearly didn't like reporters! All the same, his reaction had really been right over the top. Grabbing hold of her and throwing her into this cellar—no one in their right mind would do something like that, no matter how much they hated the Press!

Anyway, why would a reporter be interested in this place? Was the man famous, or something? Rose certainly hadn't recognised him.

'Never mind who he is,' she reminded herself. 'That isn't important right now. Just concentrate on getting *out* of here.'

But getting out wasn't going to be easy. In fact, it didn't take her long to realise that it was downright impossible. She was going to have to stay here until that man came to his senses and let her out.

And how long was that going to take? Rose had no idea. She huddled at the top of the steps again, and wished she were wearing a thick jumper instead of a thin T-shirt and cotton skirt.

'He didn't even give me time to explain,' she muttered, scowling darkly now. 'He just grabbed me and shoved me down here. He didn't even wait to see if I really was a reporter.'

Now that she thought about it, she realised that she had smelt alcohol on his breath. '*Drunk* and crazy,' she decided uneasily. And that was a pretty dangerous combination. Perhaps she was safer down here, behind this locked door!

Time passed incredibly slowly. Rose finally left the top of the steps and went down into the cellar itself, hoping that there might be another door she had missed, some way she could get out of here. A thorough search revealed nothing, though. There was a lot of rubbish and a lot of dust, and that was it.

Thrown in among the rubbish was a chair with a broken back. Rose pulled it out and then sat on it. It left dust marks all over her skirt, but she was already fairly grubby after her exploration of the cellar. Anyway, a little dirt was the least of her worries. The only thing that interested her was, when was that man going to come back and unlock the door? And what was going to happen when he did?

Since she couldn't answer any of those questions, she simply sat and stared at the wall. Her mood kept swinging wildly between fierce anger and sharp waves of fear. After a while, she couldn't sit still any longer, and she began to pace up and down.

'It's a good thing I'm not claustrophobic,' she muttered under her breath. 'Otherwise I'd be climbing the walls by now!'

What she hated almost more than anything was the sense of helplessness that she felt. She was entirely at the mercy of that man upstairs, and the worst thing of all was that she didn't know who—or what—he was. A madman, a rapist, a pervert—all sorts of frightening possibilities flashed through her mind.

'You must have been out of your mind, coming to this remote spot in answer to an advert you saw in a shop window,' she told herself more than once. 'Why on earth didn't you check up first? Try to find out something about the place—and its owner—before waltzing out here? Perhaps he only put that card in the shop because he hoped some young woman would be stupid enough to come out here on her own.'

Yet, that didn't somehow add up. He had thought she was a reporter—that was why he had been so angry. If he had simply wanted to lure a woman out here for some unpleasant purpose that she didn't even want to think about, he wouldn't have bothered with all that speech about intrusions into his privacy, and reporters being parasites.

Rose glanced at her watch and was amazed to find that it was now early evening. This was absolutely absurd, she decided angrily. How much longer was he going to keep her down here?

She climbed the stairs and began thumping on the door again. 'Look, I'm not a reporter!' she yelled. 'I came about that job you advertised. Please, just open this door and *let me out*!'

It was useless, though. She had known all along that it would be, but sheer frustration had made her try it. She wasn't even sure he could hear her through the thickness of the door.

The rest of the evening ticked away relentlessly, until the hands of her watch had finally crept right round to midnight. Rose couldn't quite believe that she had been locked in the cellar of Lyncombe Manor all this time. She was here, though, so she supposed she *had* to believe it. And she was beginning to face the horrifying realisation that he intended to keep her locked in here all night.

'He's mad as a hatter,' she whispered to herself. 'He has to be mad even to think of doing something like this!'

She was sitting on a pile of old sacking now, which was marginally more comfortable than the broken chair. She was hungry and she was thirsty, but that didn't seem very important. It was still cold in the cellar, but she didn't notice it any more. There were far more pressing worries on her mind. After a while, she realised she was biting her nails, a habit which she had developed as a child whenever she was anxious or fearful. She had grown out of it when she had reached her teens, and this was the first time she had done it in years. She made an effort to stop, but couldn't. There was something comforting about the childish habit.

The small hours of the morning began to crawl by. Rose felt as if this night were going to stretch on forever. She curled up in a small ball on the rough sacking and tried to sleep for a while, but she was too cold and too much on edge to manage more than an occasional fitful doze. Once, she found herself wondering if he *ever* intended to let her out of here. That was such a terrifying thought, though, that she quickly pushed it to the very back of her mind and wouldn't allow herself to think about it again.

Although no natural light reached the cellar, her watch finally told her that dawn was at last approaching. Rose roused herself out of the lethargy that had begun to creep over her, crawled up to the top of the steps and began hammering mechanically on the door again. Unless he let her out of here soon—*very* soon—she was absolutely certain that she was going to start falling apart.

A few minutes later, to her intense relief, she heard the sound of the door being unlocked. Just the prospect of freedom gave her new courage and energy. He *wasn't* going to find her huddled on the floor, looking cowed and close to a gibbering wreck. She even made an effort to run her fingers through her hair, to restore it to some kind of order.

The door swung open, and the man stood there looking down at her with a slightly blank expression on his face.

'You've been here all night?' he said, a little disbelievingly.

Rose's violet eyes flared furiously. 'It's rather hard to walk through a locked door!'

'I forgot you were down here.'

'You *forgot*?' she repeated, on a rising note of sheer anger. 'How on earth could you forget you'd locked someone in the cellar?'

'Please don't shout,' he said in a tired voice. 'I've got a hell of a hangover this morning.'

'Oh, I really am sorry to hear that,' Rose retorted. 'I do apologise if I'm making your headache worse.'

'Look, I realise you're upset over this——'

'Upset!' she yelled at him. 'That doesn't even begin to describe the way I feel right now!'

She saw him visibly wince at the shrillness of her voice, and was pleased that she was managing to hurt him in some way.

'What happened was entirely your own fault,' he said tersely. 'I didn't ask you to come here.'

'Oh, but you did,' Rose told him, and was very gratified by his sudden change of expression.

'What do you mean by that?' he asked abruptly.

But Rose was beginning to shift around rather restlessly. It had been a long night, and that cellar had had very little to offer in the way of facilities.

'I need to use your bathroom,' she said in a defiant tone.

He looked as if he would like to refuse. She was sure that what he really wanted to do was to push her out of the door, and then simply forget about her. That wasn't going to happen, though. Rose was quite determined about that. By the time she had finished with him, he was *never* going to forget what he had done to her.

'There's a bathroom at the end of that passageway,' he said at last, gesturing to his right with grudging reluctance.

Rose quickly set off in the direction he had indicated. She soon found the bathroom, which was small but very clean and well equipped. She didn't see why she should hurry, and so she spent more time than was necessary washing off the dust and dirt from that cellar.

She couldn't do much about her grimy clothes, except try to sponge off the worst of the dirt. When she had done the best she could, she shook her tousled hair into place; then she studied her reflection.

'You look like someone who's just spent the night in a cellar,' she told herself with a grimace. 'And that man's definitely going to pay for his barbaric behaviour!'

Her eyes began to blaze with anger again as she left the bathroom. No one had the right to treat another human being like that, and get away with it. When she returned to the passageway where she had left him, she found the man had gone. The cellar door still stood open, and she hurriedly looked away as she walked past it. That was one place she certainly never wanted to see again!

Rose went on through to the kitchen, but there was still no sign of him. The back door stood open, and she walked through it and out into the small courtyard.

The sun was blazing down out of a clear blue sky again, and it was already quite hot. Rose wasn't in the mood to pay any attention to the weather, though. Her gaze had already swung round to rest on the man who was standing on the far side of the courtyard.

She walked directly over and planted herself right in front of him. His eyes—which were slate-grey—rested on her without much interest.

'I thought you'd gone,' he said, his tone clearly telling her that he wished she *had* gone. As far as he was concerned, she was just a nuisance. He wanted to be rid of her as quickly as possible.

'No, I haven't gone,' Rose replied in a taut voice. 'You see, before I leave, there are a couple of things that I want you to know. Firstly, I am not a reporter. And secondly, as soon as I do leave here, I intend to go straight to the police and report exactly what you did to me.'

She was rather annoyed to find that he didn't seem in the least perturbed by her threat.

'If you're not a reporter, why did you come here yesterday?' he asked her.

'You put a card in one of the local shops, advertising for a gardener. I came to Lyncombe Manor because I wanted to apply for the job.'

His dark eyebrows gently rose. 'You don't look like a gardener to me.'

'Gardeners don't have to be old men with cloth caps and green fingers,' she retorted. 'I know about plants, I'm strong enough to handle a lawnmower and dig flower-beds, and I'm not afraid of hard work.'

To her surprise, a glimmer of amusement briefly showed in those slate-grey eyes.

'I get the feeling that you're not afraid of anything much at all,' he commented. 'All right, you can have the job.'

For a few seconds, Rose just stared at him, hardly able to believe that he had just said that.

'Do you really think I want your lousy job any more?' she said incredulously, at last. 'As far as I'm concerned, you're more than a little crazy. No one in their right mind would even think of doing what you did yesterday. And there's no way I'd ever work for someone like you!'

Her outburst seemed to leave him completely unmoved. Instead, he merely shrugged. 'Then there's not a lot more I can say.'

Rose drew herself up to her full height, which was a fairly impressive five feet, eight inches, and glared straight into his irritatingly expressionless features.

'I should think there's a great deal more you can say,' she hissed at him. 'You haven't even *apologised* for what you did.'

He met her gaze unblinkingly. 'I've already explained that leaving you down there all night was just an unfortunate mistake. I meant to lock you in for an hour or two, no more. I had a little too much to drink yesterday, though. I fell asleep and forgot about you.'

Her own eyes glittered back at him. 'Well, I intend to make you very sorry that you've got such a bad memory!'

He gave a resigned sigh. 'All right, what is it going to take to put this right? Money?' He pulled a cheque-book out of his pocket. 'How much is this going to cost me?'

'A great deal,' she threw back at him with fierce anger. 'And you're not going to be able to buy your way out of it with a big cheque!'

With that, she turned her back on him and walked angrily out of the courtyard.

She glanced round only once, to see if he was following her. She was suddenly frightened in case he decided that he didn't intend to let her go. He hadn't moved an inch, though. He was still standing on the far side of the courtyard, a man who was lean to the point of thinness, his dark hair shaggy and in need of a good cut, and his slate-grey eyes curiously expressionless.

For just a moment, Rose's gaze locked on to his, and her skin suddenly prickled in an odd way, as if something were warning her to be very careful of this man. Don't worry, she told herself grimly. I've no intention of setting eyes on him again—unless it's in a court of law!

She turned away from him again, hurried round the side of the house and made her way towards her car. To her relief, it started first time. She crunched it into gear, trod hard on the accelerator and roared away from Lyncombe Manor. And she had no intention of ever coming back.

A quarter of an hour later, Rose pulled up outside the small house where she was staying for bed and breakfast. Mrs Rogers, who owned and ran it, opened the door as she walked up the front path.

'I've been so worried about you,' she said, her face creased into anxious lines. 'When you didn't come back last night, I didn't know what to do. At first, I wondered if I ought to call the police. Then I thought you might have met someone, and—well—decided you wanted to spend some time with him,' she finished tactfully. 'I'm ever so relieved to see you, and know you're all right.' Then she saw the dishevelled and grubby state of Rose's clothes, and an anxious look crossed her face again. 'You *are* all right, aren't you?'

'Well, I'm not hurt,' Rose assured her. 'But I'm definitely not all right,' she added, with a dark scowl.

'Come on inside,' said Mrs Rogers. 'I'll make you a cup of tea, and you can tell me all about it.'

Rose let herself be ushered into the kitchen, where Mrs Rogers clucked over the state of her while she bustled round making the tea. Rose had sometimes found Mrs Rogers' motherliness a little irritating during the couple of weeks she had been staying here. This morning, though, she was rather glad of it. She felt badly in need of a little kindness and attention.

'Where have you been since yesterday?' asked Mrs Rogers, as she poured out the tea. 'Not that I want to pry into your private affairs,' she added hastily. 'But I worry about you, a young woman travelling around all on your own. And I expect your parents can't sleep at night, wondering what's happening to you.'

'I dare say my parents sleep very well,' Rose said drily. 'They always think I'm quite capable of looking after myself. And usually I am. But then, I don't usually run into the sort of man I met yesterday.'

Mrs Rogers eyes instantly gleamed. 'A man?' she echoed. She loved gossip of any kind. 'I thought it would turn out to be something like that. Whenever there's any kind of trouble, it's nearly always a man who's the cause of it.'

'Well, this particular man certainly caused me enough trouble!' Rose said darkly. 'And as soon as I've finished this drink and had a bath, I'm going straight to the police.'

'The police?' breathed Mrs Rogers. 'Good heavens! Whatever did he do?'

'He kept me locked in a cellar all night! You see, I went to Lyncombe Manor to apply for this job——'

'Lyncombe Manor?' interrupted Mrs Rogers. 'Where that nice Mr Hayward lives?'

Rose looked at her in surprise. 'You know Lyncombe Manor?'

'I've never been there,' Mrs Rogers told her. 'But my brother—he's a plumber—went there a couple of weeks ago to do some work. Something to do with the boiler, I think. When he came round to see me last week, he told me who lived there. Of course, he made me promise I wouldn't tell anyone. Mr Hayward likes his privacy. I suppose he's had enough of reporters and the Press, and you can understand that.'

Rose was thoroughly confused by this time. 'I don't think I understand anything of this at all,' she said, with a touch of exasperation. 'And who is this "nice Mr Hayward"? I'm sure it can't be the same man I met yesterday!'

'He writes songs,' said Mrs Rogers. 'At first, I didn't recognise the name either. Then my brother told me some of the songs he's written, and I knew quite a lot of them. And of course, I knew that pretty blonde girl he used to write for, only they've split up now—in fact, about a year ago it was. And there was such a lot about it in the papers, week after week it went on, so it's hardly surprising Mr Hayward got sick of it, and went in hiding from the Press.'

Rose was still trying to take all of this in. 'Are you talking about Nathan Hayward? The songwriter? *The* Nathan Hayward?'

'That's him,' agreed Mrs Rogers. 'I thought you'd know the name. He's quite famous, really.' Then a small frown crossed her face. 'But why did he lock you in the cellar?' she asked in a puzzled voice. 'That doesn't sound like the kind of thing Mr Hayward would do. My brother was quite impressed by him. Said he didn't say a lot, but he let my brother get on with the job without any interference, and paid his bill very promptly—which is more than a lot of people do,' she added in a disapproving tone.

Rose felt the colour rise in her face. She already owed Mrs Rogers some money for her food and board, and right now she didn't have any spare cash.

'Oh, I didn't mean you, dear,' Mrs Rogers said quickly, seeing Rose's embarrassment. 'I know you'll let me have the money as soon as you've got it.'

'I'm trying very hard to get a job,' Rose assured her. 'In fact, that's why I went to Lyncombe Manor. Only Mr Hayward—well, I suppose it was Mr Hayward—caught me looking round the house, and he thought I was a reporter.'

'Well, I expect that would explain his behaviour, if he didn't treat you very well,' said Mrs Rogers. 'A lot of things they said about him in the newspapers weren't at all nice. If I were him, I wouldn't be at all polite to someone I thought was from the Press.'

'But he shut me in the cellar!' said Rose, with a quick surge of her old indignation. 'And then he forgot I was there. He left me there all night!'

'That wasn't a very nice thing to do,' agreed Mrs Rogers. 'But I think the poor man has had rather a bad time. People often behave quite badly when they've had a lot of upsetting things to cope with.'

Rose thought that Mrs Rogers probably wouldn't be so charitable if *she* had been the one who had been locked in the cellar. All the same, she was beginning to see the whole thing from a slightly different point of view. That didn't excuse his behaviour, of course— *nothing* could do that, as far as she was concerned—

but it did explain his pathological dislike of anyone he suspected of being a reporter.

Nathan Hayward—Rose was rather out of touch with the current music scene, but his name was definitely familiar. He wrote beautiful songs that sounded deceptively simple, but in fact had complex underlying harmonies that always made her nerve-ends tingle responsively whenever she heard them.

She hadn't recognised him when she'd seen him, but that was hardly surprising. He had been the background figure in his partnership with Jancis Kendall, the 'pretty blonde girl' Mrs Rogers had mentioned. As a team of songwriter and singer, they had made a small fortune and sold records all round the world. Until just over a year ago, that was, when they had split up in a great blaze of publicity. Nathan Hayward had seemed to disappear from sight soon afterwards. Only it seemed he hadn't vanished completely. He was at Lyncombe Manor, just a couple of miles from here...

'Are you still going to the police?' asked Mrs Rogers, a little anxiously. She obviously didn't want to get too involved with any resulting unpleasantness.

'I don't know,' said Rose slowly. 'I need to think about this.' She got to her feet, still trying to take it all in. 'If it's all right with you, I'll go up and take a bath.'

'Have a good long soak,' advised Mrs Rogers. 'You'll feel much better afterwards.'

After a hot bath and a change of clothes, Rose certainly looked much better. She was still very mixed-up inside, though. And she hadn't stopped being angry at that man—no, she couldn't call him that any more, she reminded herself. He had a name, now. Nathan

Hayward. A name she knew. A man who was exceptionally talented, and whose songs she had always enjoyed and admired.

Yet, he had locked her in a cellar *all night*. Should he be allowed to get away with that?

Of course not, Rose told herself firmly. But what could she do about it? Now that she had calmed down, she really didn't want to go to the police. That had been just a spur-of-the-moment reaction. What alternative was there, though?

She finally decided that there was only one thing she could do. That was, to go and see him again. Perhaps she would feel better if she got a proper apology out of him, instead of just a rather weary show of indifference.

She conveniently forgot that she had sworn that she would never set foot in Lyncombe Manor again. At the same time, she was willing to admit that she was rather curious to see Nathan Hayward just one more time, now that she knew who he was.

One short visit, she told herself. I'll stay just long enough to make him apologise; then I'll put this whole thing behind me. I'll forget it ever happened.

And she honestly thought she would be able to do that.

CHAPTER TWO

ROSE decided to go to Lyncombe Manor that same afternoon, while she could still remember how very angry she had been at Nathan Hayward's completely uncivilised behaviour. If she left it another day, she might calm down completely. Worse than that, she might even act like a rather star-struck teenager when she finally came face to face with him. She definitely didn't want that to happen!

She set off after lunch, although she very nearly changed her mind at the last moment. Something seemed to be warning her that it wasn't at all a good idea to go back to Lyncombe Manor.

If she stayed away, though, it would mean that Nathan Hayward would get away with the outrageous way he had treated her. And Rose didn't intend to let him get away with it. She lifted her head with new determination and headed the car in the direction of Nathan Hayward's beautiful house.

The narrow, winding lane that led to it was just as deserted as it had been the day before. The sun was blazing down again—it looked as if a long spell of hot, dry weather was setting in—and Rose wound down the car windows, and pushed back her thick mop of hair.

When she finally reached Lyncombe Manor, she was struck all over again by its picturesque charm. The roses seemed to be blooming even more brightly and prolifically than yesterday, and their scent drifted towards her on the warm, balmy air as she got out of the car.

The house itself looked as deserted as it had on her last visit, but Rose wasn't fooled this time. She had made the mistake of thinking it empty once before— she wasn't about to do it again!

Nor did she make any effort to walk round to the back of the house. Instead, she marched firmly up to the front door and thumped loudly on the heavy knocker.

No one opened the door and there wasn't a sound from inside the house. Rose frowned. Perhaps he really *was* out this time. She hammered on the knocker once more; then she stood back and looked up at the windows.

As they had been the day before, they were closed, despite the heat of the day. The man didn't just live like a recluse—it looked as if he wasn't even very fond of fresh air and sunshine!

She began to walk slowly away from the house, aware of an unexpected sense of disappointment. She knew she wouldn't come back again. Unless she carried out her threat to go to the police—and, by now, she was fairly certain that she wouldn't do that— Nathan Hayward would get off scot-free.

An unexpected sound interrupted her thoughts and made her come to a stop. Her brows drew lightly together. What had it been? And where had it come from?

She was just beginning to think that perhaps she had imagined it when it came again. And this time, she realised at once what it was. It was someone shouting.

Although she couldn't be certain, it seemed to come from the back of the house. And she didn't want to go round *there* again! That maniac might jump out, accuse her of trespassing, and bundle her back into the cellar!

She heard the shout ring out for the third time, and gave a small sigh. She supposed she couldn't just walk away until she had found out what was going on.

Keeping her eyes carefully peeled for any sign of Nathan Hayward, she cautiously made her way under the arch at the side of the house; then she headed towards the gardens at the back. She still couldn't see anyone, and the shouting seemed to have stopped now. The grounds stretched out in front of her, wildly overgrown and yet still beautiful, while behind her was the small courtyard, with its tubs of ferns and its air of tranquillity.

'Hey, you down there!' shouted a familiar voice. 'I need a hand.'

Rose nearly jumped out of her skin as the voice echoed round the courtyard. Her head jerked up, and her eyes squinted a little as she stared at the figure silhouetted against the bright sunlight that blazed down on to the roof.

Then her gaze returned to the courtyard. There was a ladder lying on the ground on the far side. She realised that it must have fallen down—leaving Nathan Hayward stranded on the roof!

She took a few steps back, and shaded her eyes as she looked up again, so that she could see him better.

He was perched on the sloping roof above the kitchen, and he was scowling darkly.

'You!' he said, as he recognised her.

'Me,' agreed Rose, her mouth gradually relaxing into a satisfied grin as she realised that she was certainly in no danger from Nathan Hayward at the moment. She sauntered over to the wooden bench she had sat on yesterday, and comfortably seated herself. 'You look as if you need some help,' she commented.

His scowl deepened. 'Instead of stating the obvious, why not put that ladder back against the wall, so I can get down?' he said tersely.

'I didn't hear you say "please".' Rose was beginning to get a lot of satisfaction from this situation.

'That's because I didn't say it!' Then he seemed to become aware that he was the one who was at a distinct disadvantage at the moment. 'I would be grateful if you would replace that ladder,' he said in a taut voice, obviously finding it a great effort to be even faintly civil.

'It was very careless of you to let it fall in the first place,' Rose observed. 'Anyway, what are you doing up there?'

'Replacing a couple of slates. When I went to get down, my foot slipped, and I kicked the ladder away.'

Rose clucked her tongue. 'How unfortunate. And now you're stuck up there,' she added, her violet eyes beginning to gleam a little. 'You're really very lucky I turned up. You could have been up there for hours.'

'I heard someone knocking at the front door, and so I shouted out,' he growled. 'I hoped whoever it was would hear me. Of course, I didn't know it was you.'

'You probably didn't expect to see me again.'

'I certainly didn't!'

Rose relaxed back on the bench. She was beginning to enjoy this very much.

'Do you know why I came back here?' she asked him.

'No, I don't. And frankly, I'm not interested. I simply want to get down from here.'

Rose ignored his rudeness. 'I came back because it occurred to me that you owed me an apology. In fact, you owe me a lot more than that, considering what you did to me. But I think I'd probably settle for a really full and comprehensive apology.'

Nathan Hayward glared down at her. Even from this distance, she could see the steely colour of his eyes, and knew that he was hating every moment of this. Good! she thought with some glee. She had never thought she would have an opportunity like this to get her own back, and she intended to make the most of it.

'Is that what I've got to do before you'll help me to get down?' he demanded. 'Give you a grovelling apology?'

Rose's gaze became very cool again. 'Do you know what last night was like for me?' she demanded. 'Shut in that cellar for all those hours by someone I didn't know, not having the slightest idea when—or even if— I was ever going to get out? Or what you were going to do to me when you *did* let me out?'

'Don't over-dramatise the whole thing,' he said irritably.

'Over-dramatise?' she echoed incredulously. 'I don't think I've over-dramatised anything! What you did was quite literally criminal. You could go to gaol for it!'

'All right, it was a pretty stupid thing to do. I admit that,' he conceded grudgingly. 'And I apologise for it.'

From the tone of his voice, Rose knew perfectly well that he didn't mean a word of it. He didn't regret it at all. He was simply saying what he thought she wanted to hear, because he wanted to get down off that roof. And he couldn't do that without her help.

Well, right now Nathan Hayward was about the last person on earth whom she felt like helping!

Rose got to her feet and glared up at him. 'I think it's about time that someone taught you that you can't do whatever you like, and get away with it. Last night, I needed you to unlock that door and let me out, but you were so drunk that you didn't even remember that you'd locked me in there! Now, you need me to put that ladder back up against the wall, so you can get down. Well, shall I tell you what I intend to do, Mr Hayward? I'm going to go away and forget about *you* for a while. It might be an hour, a couple of hours— or I might put you right out of my mind until the morning. Do you fancy a night up on the roof?' she enquired sweetly. 'You might be lucky, and it'll be a warm, dry night. Or *I* might be lucky, and the weather will turn cold and wet. However it turns out, I hope you'll be thoroughly uncomfortable until I decide that I feel like coming back again.'

He swore at her with soft venom, and Rose looked up at him with deep antipathy.

'I don't like men who use bad language. In fact, I don't like you, Mr Hayward! And perhaps you'd better not do anything to make me dislike you even more than I do already, or I might not come back at all.'

With that parting shot, she stalked out of the courtyard, not even glancing round for one last look at him. It had been a spur-of-the-moment decision to leave him up there, prompted by his unpleasant attitude and by her own still vivid memories of last night. It would be a very long time before she forgot those long, miserable and often panicky hours she had spent in that cellar.

She had no idea how long she planned to leave him up there. Of course, she would come back eventually. She hadn't actually meant it when she had threatened not to come back at all. He wouldn't know that, though. At least, she hoped he wouldn't. She wanted him to sweat for a while—quite a *long* while. Rose wasn't usually vindictive by nature. In fact, she had never reacted to anyone quite as violently as she had to Nathan Hayward. But then, no one had ever treated her the way he had!

She got into her car, determined to drive off and forget about him for a while, just as she had threatened. She even started up the engine and got a couple of hundred yards down the lane. Then she stopped the car again.

A deep sigh escaped her. It was no good. She couldn't do this. At the time, he had made her so mad that she had really believed she could go through with it. Her bursts of temper never lasted for very long, though. This one was already dying away, leaving a feeling of guilt to take its place.

Why on earth should you feel guilty? she asked herself in exasperation. Leaving him sitting on a roof for a while on a hot, sunny afternoon wasn't all that dreadful, was it? It certainly wasn't as bad as spending the night in a cold, dirty cellar!

She sat and stared rigidly out of the window for another few minutes, stubbornly fighting her sudden attack of conscience. It was no good. In the end, her

conscience won—in fact, she had known all along that
it would. With another sigh, she restarted the engine,
turned the car round, and headed back towards
Lyncombe Manor.

Her feet dragged as she made her way back round
the house to that sheltered courtyard. She hated giving
in so quickly, but at the same time she knew she
couldn't deliberately leave him up there any longer.

When she finally reached the courtyard, she looked
up at the roof with great reluctance. She could just
imagine how unbearably smug he would look when
he realised that she had come back already.

He wasn't there, though. At least, not where she
had left him. There wasn't any figure silhouetted
against the sunlight, impatiently waiting for her to
return. Her gaze slid over the stretches of roof on
either side, but he wasn't there, either. Where on earth
was he? The ladder was still lying on the ground, so
no one else had come along and put it up for him.
Anyway, she would have seen anyone approaching the
manor.

Then she suddenly gave an enormous gulp and her
heart actually seemed to stop for a moment. Lying in
a deep patch of shade at the foot of the kitchen wall
was a sprawled figure. And it wasn't moving.

'The stupid, *stupid* man,' Rose muttered shakily
under her breath as she ran over. He hadn't been prepared to wait until she came back. Instead, he had
tried to get down without the ladder, and had fallen.

She dropped to her knees beside him, and nervously felt for a pulse in his wrist. She nearly pan-
icked completely when she couldn't find it. She tried
again, and let out a ragged sigh of relief when she
finally felt a light thumping against her fingertips. At

least he was alive. She didn't know how badly hurt
he was, though, or if anything was broken. Rose's
knowledge of first aid was very elementary. Anyway,
she knew this was a job for the experts.

She left Nathan Hayward lying sprawled on the
cobbled floor of the courtyard, and rushed into the
house. She dashed through the kitchen and along the
passageway, not even glancing at that hated cellar door
as she passed it, and finally found herself in a narrow,
stone-flagged entrance hall. There was an old-
fashioned coat-stand and a small, heavy table, but no
telephone.

Rose groaned. What if there wasn't any phone at
Lyncombe Manor? She pushed open a heavy door on
the far side of the hall and found herself in a large
room with an oak-beamed ceiling, a huge fireplace,
and a lot of ornate wood panelling. She didn't take
any notice of her surroundings, though. Her gaze had
already fixed on the phone that stood on the table.

Her shaking fingers dialled the emergency number.
When it was answered a few seconds later, she croaked
out her request for an ambulance. When she had given
brief details of where she was and why she wanted it,
she put down the phone again and raced back to the
courtyard.

Nathan Hayward hadn't moved. He was lying on
his side, so she could see his face, which looked wor-
ryingly pale. She didn't dare move him, in case he had
any broken bones, and there wasn't really anything
she could do to make him more comfortable. Instead,
she just hovered anxiously, hoping it wouldn't take
the ambulance too long to get here.

It seemed absolutely ages before she heard the sound
of the siren in the distance, although afterwards she

realised that it hadn't actually been very long at all. She rushed round to meet the ambulance, and then guided the two men with a stretcher round to the courtyard.

'Fell off the roof, did he?' asked one of the men, as he knelt down and began to run expert fingers over Nathan Hayward's body, searching for any obvious signs of injury.

'He was mending some broken slates,' Rose said in a shaky voice.

'That's a job that's best left to the experts,' observed the ambulanceman. Then he stood up, and nodded to his partner.

'Is he all right?' Rose asked falteringly. 'I mean— are there any really serious injuries?'

'Not as far as I can tell,' replied the ambulanceman, to her intense relief. 'But there could be internal injuries, of course, or fractures that will only show up on X-rays. We'll know more once we get him to hospital. Do you want to come in the ambulance with him, or follow behind in your car?'

'Oh—do I really have to come?' she said with dismay. She was already far more involved in Nathan Hayward's life than she had ever meant to be. She wasn't at all sure that she wanted it to go any further.

They were loading Nathan carefully on to the stretcher now, and one of the ambulancemen looked up at her a little disapprovingly.

'You are his wife, aren't you?' he said.

'Certainly not,' Rose replied at once.

'A relative, then.'

'No. Just—well, a sort of acquaintance. Not even that, really. In fact, I hardly know him.'

'Well, he's going to need someone,' said the ambulanceman in a more practical tone of voice. 'He might need things fetched to the hospital, and there could be people who have to be contacted if his injuries turn out to be worse than they look. And you seem to be the only person around.'

Rose gave a faint grimace. What she really wanted was to drive away from Lyncombe Manor, leaving Nathan Hayward and his problems far behind. She was already deeply regretting coming back here in the first place.

On the other hand, she couldn't help feeling rather guilty about the entire situation. After all, she *had* left him stranded up on that roof. If she had replaced the ladder, as he had asked her to do, none of this would ever have happened.

Of course, if Nathan Hayward hadn't locked her in that cellar, she would never have been tempted to leave him up on that roof in the first place. So, all of this was actually his fault, not hers. If she wanted to drive off and just forget about all this, she would be perfectly justified.

Except that she couldn't do it. Rose knew that it was perfectly ridiculous to feel worried about someone who had treated her so abominably, but he looked so helpless, lying there on that stretcher. Only someone who was really hard-hearted would be able to walk away and leave him.

'All right, I'll follow you to the hospital in my own car,' she said in a resigned voice.

Nathan was loaded into the ambulance, which then drove off with its lights flashing. Rose followed along close behind, and still couldn't quite believe that all of this was really happening. She had gone to

Lyncombe Manor to demand an apology from Nathan Hayward, and had ended up in the middle of a major emergency.

At the hospital, she was directed to a waiting-room, where she spent a nerve-racking couple of hours waiting for news. It was very late in the afternoon now, and she was tired, hungry and edgy. A tasteless cup of coffee from a vending machine didn't make her feel any better, and her nerves jumped twitchingly when she saw a man in a white coat finally heading in her direction.

'Did you come in with Mr Hayward?' he asked her.

'Yes, I did,' Rose said a little breathlessly. 'How is he? Has he come round yet?'

'He came round only minutes after he arrived. He's an extremely lucky man. As far as we can tell, his injuries are all minor. Heavy bruising, mainly—he's going to feel very stiff and sore for a few days. We would like to keep him in overnight, for observation, but he refuses to stay.'

From the doctor's tone of voice, Rose guessed that Nathan wasn't proving to be a very co-operative patient.

'Then you're letting him go home?' she said.

'We don't have a lot of choice. We can't force him to stay. He should have someone with him for the next twenty-four hours, though, in case there are any after-effects from the fall.'

'What sort of after-effects?' Rose asked nervously.

The doctor shrugged. 'Shock affects different people in different ways. If there are any severe headaches, nausea, or blackouts, he'll need to be re-admitted straight away. Ring us immediately, and we'll send an ambulance.'

'But——' Rose had been about to say that she couldn't possibly stay with him, she didn't even *know* him, but the doctor was already hurrying off in response to an urgent signal from one of the nurses. 'Oh, this is ridiculous!' she muttered in exasperation. 'How on earth did I get mixed up in all of this?'

A couple of minutes later, the door to the waiting-room opened and Nathan came in. He was sitting in a wheelchair that was being pushed by a large, cheerful-looking orderly, and he had a black scowl on his face.

'I can walk,' he growled at the orderly.

'As soon as you're outside the hospital, you can run a marathon if you want to,' said the orderly in an unruffled voice. 'But while you're inside the hospital, you're our responsibility, so you'll stay in that wheelchair. Now, where's the young lady who's going to take you home?'

Rose stepped forward. 'That's me,' she said in a very reluctant voice.

Nathan glared at her. Then he turned his head and looked up at the orderly. 'I don't want to go with her. Why can't I have an ambulance?'

'Because they've better things to do than to act as a taxi service when you've got your own transport waiting for you,' replied the orderly, his tone pleasant but very firm. He was obviously used to dealing with difficult patients.

Nathan scowled darkly again, but subsided into silence. Rose didn't know if he was a little ashamed of behaving so badly, or just didn't feel well enough to argue any more. He certainly looked very white, and, from the way he occasionally shifted uncomfortably in the wheelchair, she guessed that his bruises were already beginning to make themselves felt.

The orderly wheeled him out, and Rose followed close behind. Once they had left the hospital, Rose led them over to her car. Nathan stiffly levered himself out of the wheelchair and eased himself into the front seat of the car, impatiently shaking off the orderly when he attempted to help him.

'Right,' said the orderly, with a sympathetic glance at Rose, 'he's all yours now.'

'Thanks very much,' muttered Rose, getting into the car beside Nathan as the orderly pushed away the empty wheelchair.

Nathan stared rigidly out of the front window. He seemed determined to ignore her, and Rose suddenly lost her temper. The last twenty-four hours had been pretty traumatic and it was nearly all entirely his fault. Yet he was being completely boorish and behaving as if *she* were the one to blame. Well, she had had enough!

'If there's one thing I can't stand, it's people who sulk,' she said, her violet eyes flashing. 'All right, so you fell off the roof and hurt yourself. But that was *your* fault, not mine. No one asked you to try and get down from that roof without a ladder!'

'Actually, I was just thinking that I've put you to a great deal of trouble,' said Nathan, to her total surprise.

His sudden change of attitude briefly threw her. Her temper was still flaring, though. 'Yes, you have! And I don't know why you're suddenly being so polite. You certainly didn't seem very pleased to see me in that hospital. I waited all afternoon to make sure you were all right, and all you could do was be very rude both to me and that orderly.'

'I know,' agreed Nathan, surprising her all over again. 'Maybe I've been living on my own for too long. I've forgotten how to be polite to people. And on top of that, I hate hospitals. It's childish to be afraid of them, I suppose, but I can't help it, they really get to me.'

'Is that why you wouldn't stay overnight?'

'If I'd been conscious when that ambulance came, I'd have refused to get into it,' he said with a grimace.

'Why do you feel like that?'

He shrugged. 'No particular reason that I know of. A lot of people have the same sort of phobia. There's not much you can do about it—except try to stay healthy!'

'And not fall off any roofs,' she added tartly. She was no longer cross with him, though. She rarely stayed angry for very long. 'That was a pretty stupid thing to do,' she went on, 'trying to get down without a ladder. I wouldn't have left you up there for long, you know.'

'From the look on your face, I thought you planned to leave me up there all night,' he said drily.

'I was awfully tempted,' she admitted. 'But I'd never actually have done it.'

'I would have deserved it,' Nathan Hayward said, with unexpected frankness. 'Locking you in that cellar and then forgetting that you were there—it was a fairly bizarre thing to do. Believe it or not, I don't usually treat women like that.'

'I think I'd prefer to believe it,' Rose said rather fervently. 'Otherwise, I wouldn't feel very safe sitting in this car with you.'

She was amazed that she was having this comparatively civilised conversation with Nathan Hayward. They had barely said a polite word to each other since they had first met, and now he had suddenly started behaving like a normal human being. It was also a little unnerving, because she hadn't realised that he was capable of radiating an almost palpable charm. Careful! she warned herself. Remember the other side to him. Don't be fooled by the sheep's clothing. This man is definitely still a wolf!

She started up the car, driving carefully as she left the hospital car park. Although he didn't once complain, she was sure that every small bump in the road was sending jolts of pain through Nathan's bruised body.

When Rose eventually brought the car to a halt on the gravel drive at the front of Lyncombe Manor, he gave a grunt of relief.

'That's a journey that I'd prefer not to make again until some of these bruises have gone down!' He opened the car door, but then paused and turned to her. 'Sorry—I forgot to thank you for the lift. And for waiting all that time at the hospital.'

'If you carry on being so polite, I'll begin to think that fall affected you in more ways than one!' she said tartly. 'You've been a changed man since you came out of that hospital.'

'Perhaps I just wanted you to see the better side of my character. I do have one,' he said lightly.

'Hmm,' muttered Rose, a little disbelievingly. This wasn't the time to argue about it, though. Instead, she scrambled out of the car and went round to the passenger side. 'Come on,' she said more briskly, 'I'll give you a hand into the house. You'll probably feel better after you've had some rest.'

Nathan didn't make any effort to get out of the car, though. And he ignored the hand she stretched out towards him, ready to help him to his feet. 'I can manage on my own,' he told her. 'You can leave me here—I'm perfectly capable of looking after myself.'

'I dare say you are,' Rose agreed. 'But the doctor said you had to have someone with you for the next twenty-four hours. I definitely didn't want to volunteer for the job, but you don't seem to have anyone else who cares what happens to you.'

His slate-grey eyes fixed on her with a suddenly curious expression. 'And you do?'

'No,' said Rose, just a little too quickly. 'And if you treat everyone the way you treated me, I can see *why* you don't have any friends. But I can't simply walk off and leave you. If anything happened to you, I'd never be able to sleep at night again.'

'Nothing's going to happen to me,' he said with some certainty. 'And I don't need a temporary nurse.'

'I'm not volunteering to *be* one,' Rose retorted. 'I'm just going to hang around for a while, to make sure you don't get any after-effects from that fall. If you suddenly collapse or black out, you'll need someone to telephone for help.'

'I'm not going to collapse,' he growled impatiently. 'I'm going to take myself off to bed for a few hours. When I get up in the morning, I'll have a few painful bruises, but otherwise I'll be fine.'

'There's always a chance you might not be,' she said stubbornly. 'And what would you do then? I mean, you do live here all on your own, don't you?'

'Yes.' He looked at her with sudden wariness. 'And that's the way I like it,' he warned.

'I'm not planning to move in,' Rose told him with some exasperation. 'In fact, I should think you're the last person in the world that anyone would want to live with. I don't even *want* to stay overnight. The doctor said that someone has to keep an eye on you for the next few hours, though. Since I feel sort of responsible for your accident, I guess that person has got to be me.'

'You feel responsible?' he echoed, raising one eyebrow. 'Because you wouldn't put back that ladder?'

'Yes,' she admitted with some reluctance. Then her violet eyes took on a defiant glow. 'Although I don't know why *I* should feel guilty. You're the one who started all this, by locking me in that cellar.'

Nathan began to look impatient again. 'Do we really have to go over all that for the umpteenth time? I've said I'm sorry and I've tried to explain why I did it. And as for all this rubbish about feeling guilty— you're not responsible for my accident. I slipped and fell, that was all.'

'Maybe so. It doesn't make any difference, though. You've got to have someone around for a while, and it looks as if I'm the only one idiotic enough to volunteer.'

Nathan let out a heavy sigh. 'You're very persistent, aren't you?'

Rose shrugged. 'I don't really know. Once I've made my mind up about something, I hardly ever change it. Does that make me persistent?'

'It certainly seems like it to me,' he said drily. 'If you stay here overnight, won't someone miss you? Don't you have people expecting you home?'

'I'm on sort of a prolonged holiday,' Rose explained. 'I'm staying at a guest house at the moment. I can easily ring Mrs Rogers—she owns and runs it— and explain that I won't be back until tomorrow.'

He was looking at her steadily now, and for the first time there was a faint flicker of curiosity in his grey eyes.

'You're an odd girl,' he said at last. 'You turn up out of the blue, you insist on sticking around to help me, even though I treated you in a way that would have most girls running off and screaming for the police, and you don't seem to have anyone much who cares if you suddenly decide to spend the night at the house of a stranger.'

Rose shook her head. 'You're wrong about that. I've got a lot of family and friends who care about me. It's just that most of them are rather a long way away. Perhaps you're mixing me up with yourself,' she went on steadily. '*You're* the one who lives like a recluse, and doesn't seem to want anyone to share even a small part of your life.'

For a few moments, their gazes met and held. Then Nathan's grey eyes took on a bleak tinge, and he looked away. 'I don't want to talk any more,' he muttered. 'It's making my head ache. Let's get into the house.'

Rose could take a hint. Anyway, she had had enough of this conversation, as well. She didn't even know what had made her say that—she certainly wasn't interested in Nathan Hayward's private life. She just wanted to get through the next few hours, and then get away from here—and from this often prickly and bad-tempered man.

Nathan got out of the car and walked very stiffly towards Lyncombe Manor. Rose trailed along a couple of paces behind, and had the feeling that she was about to make her second big mistake.

The first, of course, had been coming back here in the first place. The second was getting even further involved with this man, when it really wasn't necessary. Even now, she could change her mind and leave him. Chances were that he would be perfectly all right.

But if he wasn't? whispered a small voice inside her head. If something happened to him, wouldn't she feel badly about it for the rest of her life?

Rose gave a deep sigh, told herself that she would stay here for just the one night, and then followed Nathan Hayward into Lyncombe Manor.

CHAPTER THREE

THE sun was beginning to set, and a dark golden glow filled the interior of the house. Rose knew that, if Lyncombe Manor belonged to her, she would never want to leave it. Ever since she had first seen it, it had cast a spell on her. In fact, she thought it was one of the reasons she had come back again. She had longed to see it one more time.

Nathan walked wearily through the entrance hall, and paused at the foot of the stairs that wound up to the first floor. 'I'm going up to bed,' he told her.

'But—what should I do, now that I'm here?' asked Rose, a little awkwardly.

'The kitchen's through there,' he said, pointing towards the door at the end of the passage. 'Get yourself something to eat if you're hungry. And if you're absolutely determined to stay the night—although I've already told you it isn't necessary—there are a couple of spare bedrooms upstairs.'

With that, he hauled himself stiffly up the stairs and disappeared from sight, leaving Rose standing in the middle of the entrance hall, wondering why on earth she had decided to stay.

If you had any sense, you'd go straight home, she told herself. Except that, at the moment, home was only Mrs Rogers' guest house. It was comfortable, but quite ordinary. Not at all like Lyncombe Manor, with its wild, beautiful gardens, its rooms with stone-flagged floors and heavily beamed ceilings, and its air of mysterious secrecy.

She began to prowl quietly through the ground floor of the house, unable to resist the urge to explore. The rooms were sparsely furnished with old, ornately carved chairs, large dressers, and long, plain, oak tables. The massive fireplace in the great hall was filled with logs which wouldn't now be lit until next winter, and the only sound came from the bulky grandfather clock which ticked slowly and solemnly in the corner.

The evening light was beginning to fade to soft dusk now, and Rose switched on a couple of lamps. They cast only dim puddles of light, and the corners of the great hall were filled with shadows. In an old house like this, the atmosphere could easily have seemed quite eerie, but Rose didn't feel in the least nervous. In fact, she felt surprisingly at home. That was a little disturbing, because she was very much aware that this house belonged to Nathan Hayward. That fact alone should have made her feel uneasy about staying under this particular roof.

She realised that she was beginning to get very hungry, and so she reluctantly left the great hall and made her way to the kitchen. A quick search of the cupboards and refrigerator revealed a good supply of fresh foods, salads and vegetables. Rose hadn't expected that. Many men living on their own existed on tinned food and frozen dinners. Nathan Hayward obviously wasn't one of them.

Then she realised that she might have made a very basic mistake in assuming that he always lived alone. Just because there was no one else around at the moment, that didn't mean he lived like a monk *all* the time. Perhaps there was a girlfriend who came down occasionally. Or even girlfriends, in the plural. Nathan Hayward struck her as a man who would very easily attract women.

Yet she had the feeling that it was a very long time since a woman had set foot in Lyncombe Manor. The house gave the impression of being lived in only by a male. There were no flowers anywhere, no ornaments, or any sign that a female had had a hand in choosing the furnishings.

Rose finally gave a small shrug. It really wasn't of any interest to her whether he had a girlfriend, or even an entire harem. In fact, she had already showed far too much curiosity about Nathan Hayward's lifestyle, and it occurred to her that it might be a good idea to stop right now.

She briskly prepared a meal for herself, ate it, and then cleared away the dishes. It was fully dark outside by this time, and she caught herself yawning more than once.

'Time for bed,' she told herself. 'All you've got to do now is to find yourself an empty bedroom.'

She switched off most of the lights downstairs, leaving just one small lamp burning in the hall so she could see her way up the stairs. The first flight curved round to a small landing, and Rose let out a loud, startled yelp as a huge figure suddenly loomed out of the shadows.

A door opened on the first floor and Nathan appeared, silhouetted in the doorway. 'What the hell's going on?' he demanded irritably.

As light streamed out from his room and lit the landing, Rose gradually began to relax. At the same time, she started to feel a complete fool. The huge figure wasn't a burglar, waiting to leap out at her. It was a massive suit of armour!

'Sorry,' she muttered, looking up at Nathan sheepishly. 'Did I wake you up?'

'I've been awake for the last hour,' he told her curtly. 'Why did you shout out like that?'

'The stairs were dark—I couldn't see properly.' She pointed at the suit of armour, feeling really stupid now. 'I thought it was someone waiting to jump out at me.'

Nathan lifted one eyebrow. 'I wouldn't have let you stay here if I'd known you were of a nervous disposition. This house has a lot of spooky corners.'

'I'm never nervous,' Rose denied at once. 'Well—hardly ever,' she amended, remembering a couple of moments during the last twenty-four hours when her nerves had felt decidedly twitchy. 'Anyway, why are you awake?' she went on, deciding it was time to change the subject. 'You do feel all right, don't you?'

'As well as it's possible to feel after falling off a roof,' Nathan replied drily. 'And I'm awake because I hardly ever sleep for more than three or four hours at a stretch.'

'But it's only eleven o'clock,' Rose pointed out. 'What are you going to do for the rest of the night?'

'Do you really think that's any of your business?' he enquired, and she immediately flushed.

'No, I suppose not,' she mumbled. 'Well, I want to get some sleep, even if you don't. Which room should I use?'

He pointed to a door a little further along from his. 'You'll find a bed in there.' He walked towards the top of the stairs, and then paused for a moment. 'I'll see you in the morning—unless the ghost scares you out before the night's over.'

Rose couldn't stop herself from swallowing hard. 'Ghost?' she repeated, trying very hard to sound completely unfazed, but not quite managing it.

Nathan suddenly grinned, a wolfish smile which sent a whole swarm of goose-pimples over her skin.

'Every house as old as this has to have a ghost.'

'Have you——?' Rose cleared her throat, and tried again. 'Have you seen it?'

'Of course not,' he replied calmly. 'I don't believe in ghosts, so how could I possibly see one?'

'Then how do you know it exists?' she demanded.

'Because the previous owners told me they used to see it quite regularly. But don't worry, it doesn't wail or weep, or clank chains. It just wanders round the house very quietly, trying hard not to disturb anyone too much.'

Rose scowled at him. 'I think you're making the whole thing up! But if you're trying to scare me out of here, it isn't going to work. I don't care if half a dozen ghosts parade around my room, or even if one appears with its head tucked under its arm. I'm staying here until the morning, and even then I'm not leaving until you've convinced me you're perfectly healthy.'

With that, she flounced along to the room he had pointed out, and rather noisily closed the door.

She turned on the light switch; then her mouth opened a little in surprise. Nathan had told her she would find a bed in there—but he *hadn't* told her that it was a huge four-poster that nearly filled the entire room.

'Even for a house like this, this is a little over the top,' she muttered to herself wryly.

She sat on the edge of the bed rather gingerly, and was relieved to find that it felt very comfortable. Then she stood up again, and wondered where the nearest bathroom was.

Since she definitely didn't want to have to go and ask Nathan, she ventured back into the passageway outside, and began opening doors. The third one led into a small bathroom. With some relief, she stripped off and then stepped under the shower. The house might be old, but she was glad to see that all the conveniences seemed to be modern.

When she had finished drying herself on the towel that hung over the rail, she realised that she didn't have much choice except to put her rather crumpled clothes back on. In fact, she was going to have to sleep in them, since she didn't have any nightwear.

Then she looked thoughtfully at the towelling robe that hung on a hook on the door. She supposed it would be a bit of a cheek to borrow his clothes—but, on the other hand, it would be a lot more comfortable than sleeping in jeans and a T-shirt. Anyway, she could always wash it out in the morning, before she gave it back to him.

She slipped into the towelling robe, and then discovered that it felt rather odd to be wearing something that belonged to Nathan Hayward. 'Don't start getting fanciful,' she murmured to herself. 'It's an old towelling robe, that's all.'

She went back to the bedroom, turned off the light, and stretched out on the four-poster bed. Although she was tired, she couldn't sleep. She tossed and turned for over an hour, and then sat up in exasperation.

'What are you doing here?' she asked herself, running her fingers a little distractedly through her hair. 'You're looking after a man who doesn't *need* looking after. Never mind what the doctor said. Nathan Hayward isn't going to have any kind of relapse. He's too darned contrary to do something like that!'

She realised that she must have been a little mad in the first place to have insisted on staying here all night. Nathan Hayward didn't want her here, and, although she was still absolutely enchanted by Lyncombe Manor, she didn't feel at all at ease staying under the same roof as that man. Come to think of it, she didn't even know him. At least, not in the accepted sense of the word. If her parents knew that she was spending the night with a man she had met only a little over twenty-four hours ago, they would be pretty horrified. When she thought about it in that sense, *she* was fairly horrified. She already knew that he was capable of really bizarre behaviour. What else was he capable of?

The more she thought about it, the more panicky she became. During the bright light of day, it had seemed quite reasonable to stay here until she was sure he wasn't going to get any reaction from that fall. It was after midnight now, though, and very dark outside, which made everything seem quite different. It occurred to her that it was really quite insane to stay in this isolated house with a man who was a virtual stranger. If anything happened, who would be around to help her? No one! And that was why it would be a very good idea to get out of here right now.

She glanced at her watch. It was past midnight, but she was sure Mrs Rogers would let her back into the guest house, no matter what time she turned up on the doorstep. With sudden determination, Rose got out of bed, threw off the towelling robe and began to wriggle back into her own clothes. It took her only seconds to finish dressing. Then she left the bedroom and hurried down the stairs.

The passage that led to the kitchen was in darkness, but the kitchen door was slightly ajar, and she could see a thin beam of light shining through the crack. Was Nathan in there? she wondered uneasily. Perhaps he had come down to make himself a hot drink. Ought she to tell him that she was leaving, or just creep out? Reluctantly, she decided that she had better tell him that she was going. It seemed very rude to leave without saying a single word.

She pushed open the kitchen door, and found that Nathan was sitting at the kitchen table. Then her eyes flew wide open as she saw what he was about to do.

'Are you crazy?' she demanded incredulously, rushing into the room. She grabbed the glass of whisky that stood on the table in front of him, and poured it down the sink. Then she snatched the half-full bottle away, shoved it into the nearest cupboard and firmly shut the door. 'Don't you know that alcohol is just about the worst thing you could have right now?' she lectured him fiercely. 'Yes, of course you know it,' she went on, answering her own question. 'You're not stupid—although you do some pretty stupid things at times. So, why were you about to start drinking?'

Nathan's eyes had grown as stormy as she had ever seen them. They weren't a blank grey now, but lit with a vivid brightness that might have frightened her if she hadn't been so very angry at him.

'I couldn't sleep,' he replied in a taut voice. 'And when I can't sleep, I sometimes drink.'

'Was that what happened that night you left me locked in the cellar?' she challenged him. 'You couldn't sleep, so you drank yourself into a stupor and forgot I was even there?'

He had the grace to look slightly abashed. 'Something like that,' he muttered after a long pause, the light in his eyes dying away now, leaving the more familiar, weary expression in its place.

Rose slumped down in the chair opposite him. 'I was going to leave,' she admitted. 'That's why I came down here—to tell you that I was going.'

'It's past midnight,' he pointed out. 'Isn't that a rather funny time to walk out?'

'I didn't think you needed me any more. But now I've found you doing this, how can I possibly go? The minute I walk out that door, you'll probably take that bottle out of the cupboard and get totally drunk!'

'I was only planning on having one drink,' Nathan said drily. 'Two, at the very most. I'm trying to cure my insomnia—not commit suicide.'

'Even a single drink would be one too many,' Rose said severely. Then she looked at him through narrowed eyes. 'Are you sure you don't have a self-destructive streak? You really don't seem to take very good care of yourself.'

'For someone who's known me for a very short time, you ask a lot of extremely personal questions.'

She flushed a little. 'I suppose I do. The trouble is, you never volunteer any information. I can only find things out by actually asking.'

'And you're not slow to do that, are you?'

'Well, you can do the same, if you want to,' Rose replied rather defensively. 'Is there anything you want to ask *me*?'

Nathan settled back in his chair, his eyes resting on her levelly now. His dark hair was, as usual, rather dishevelled, and he was wearing the same jeans he had had on earlier, although with a different sweatshirt.

Not a man who troubled too much about his appearance, Rose decided wryly. Not that it made very much difference. She was beginning to realise that he was an extraordinarily attractive man, in his own individual way.

'There are a couple of questions that I'd be interested in hearing the answers to,' he told her, still looking directly at her.

Rose cleared her throat rather nervously. 'What sort of questions?'

'For a start, I'd rather like to know why you suddenly decided to creep away in the middle of the night.'

'I've already explained that. I decided you didn't need me any more. There didn't seem any point in staying on here.'

'You could have waited until morning, and left then,' he pointed out. Then a shadow of that wolfish smile touched the corners of his mouth. 'Unless, of course, you didn't feel safe with me here, at night.'

That was *exactly* the reason why she had wanted to run out on him, but there was no way Rose was ever going to admit that. Instead, she sat up very straight, and tried to look completely in control of the situation.

'That's an absolutely ridiculous suggestion,' she said, lying through her teeth. 'I just didn't realise it was so late, that was all. If I'd known it was after midnight, then of course I'd have stayed until morning.'

Nathan's eyes continued to rest on her thoughtfully. 'The grandfather clock in the hall struck midnight just before you came down,' he said at last.

'I didn't hear it,' Rose replied promptly.

'Perhaps you're a little deaf,' he said sympathetically.'That clock has a particularly loud chime. It can be heard right through the house.'

She scowled at him. 'I'm not deaf! But I *am* getting fed up with all these questions.'

'You're the one who invited me to ask them,' he reminded her. 'And I'm simply trying to find out why you suddenly decided to shoot off.' His eyes briefly gleamed. 'I just want to make sure that you're not running away because you're scared of me.'

'Absolutely not,' Rose denied at once, hoping that she was managing to sound very convincing. 'Anyway, it's a good thing I *did* come down, or you'd have sat here all night drinking yourself into oblivion!'

'I've already told you that I had no intention of doing any such thing. But even if I had, I don't see that it would have been any of your business.'

'You're right,' she agreed tartly. 'And don't worry, I won't interfere again. Just remember, *you're* the one who hates hospitals, not me. If you knock back half a bottle of whisky and end up in a coma, it'll be you who'll be rushed back there as an in-patient.'

'That's a very sobering thought—in every sense of the word,' remarked Nathan. To her astonishment, a faint smile appeared on his face. It made him look quite different. In fact, she almost forgot that, just a short time ago, she had been getting ready to rush out of the house because she was nervous about spending a night under the same roof as him.

'You don't want to discuss why you wanted to leave, and I'm pretty tired of talking about my drinking habits,' he went on. 'So, why don't we compromise, and find a safer topic of conversation?'

'Such as what?' asked Rose cautiously.

'You could begin by telling me your name.'

She blinked in astonishment. 'You don't know it?'

'You haven't told me, and so far I haven't bothered to ask,' he said equably.

'It's Rose,' she said. 'Rose Caldwell.'

'Rose,' he repeated thoughtfully. 'It doesn't suit you.'

'I know,' she agreed mournfully. 'I was a blonde-haired, blue-eyed baby, and everyone thought I was going to grow up into a fair-skinned, fair-haired English rose. Instead, my eyes turned violet and my hair darkened to brown. In the summer, I tan to the colour of a gypsy, and I'm tall and clumsy instead of cool and elegant.'

'I'm glad you're not blonde,' he said, to her surprise. Before she had a chance to ask him why, though, he went on. 'Why did you turn up on my doorstep, wanting a job as a gardener? From the look of your hands, that's not your usual line of work.'

Rose looked at her smooth, uncallused palms, and gave a small grimace. 'No, it isn't,' she agreed. 'I suppose that's one reason why it appealed to me. I fancied doing something different for a few weeks. And I do know about plants. I've always loved gardens, and growing things. And I'm strong enough to handle a lawnmower and cope with the digging.'

Nathan's eyebrows gently rose. 'You sound as if you're supplying me with a reference. Are you still interested in the job?'

'No—well, I don't think so—at least——' Annoyed with her own confusion, she shook her head. 'I'm not at all sure I want to work for a man like you,' she finished firmly.

His eyebrows rose still further. 'A man like me?'

She began to get annoyed. 'You know perfectly well what I mean!'

'A man who locks girls in cellars?' he suggested smoothly. 'A man who drinks too much, and lives entirely on his own?'

But Rose was beginning to get the measure of him now. 'I can cope with all those things,' she said firmly. 'I'm just not sure that I *want* to.'

'And until I know a little more about you, I might not even want to offer you the job,' Nathan replied, his expression totally bland now. 'I think that, nowadays, it pays to be very careful about whom you employ.'

Rose instantly bristled. 'You think I'm unreliable? Or that I couldn't do the work?'

'I'm simply saying that you turned up out of nowhere, and you still haven't told me anything about yourself, except your name. And I haven't any proof that you've even told the truth about that.'

Rose knew perfectly well that he was baiting her, and that helped her to keep a tight hold on her temper. 'I'm twenty-three years old and single,' she informed him. 'My father's in the diplomatic service, so I've spent most of my life abroad. That's why I'm here in England, for the summer. I decided it was time I saw something of the country where I was born. I saved up so I could spend a few months here, just travelling around seeing different places. Only everything's turned out to be more expensive than I expected, so

I'm running short of money. That's why I want a temporary job.' She ran out of breath at that point, so she stopped and glared at Nathan. 'Is there anything else you want to know?'

'What sort of job do you usually do?'

'For the last couple of years, I've worked as an interpreter. I speak four languages fluently, and I can get by in a handful of others. Whenever my father was posted to a different embassy, I always tried to learn the language of that country. Luckily, I seemed to pick them up fairly quickly. I suppose I've just got an ear for languages.'

'You seem to be a fairly talented lady all round,' Nathan remarked drily. 'Is there anything else you want to tell me about yourself?'

'No,' she said, very firmly. She had told him quite enough for one day. 'But I wouldn't mind knowing something about you.'

'If I remember rightly, you already know my name,' he said, and this time his eyes were a little more wary. 'That means that you know perfectly well who I am. And you probably know quite a lot about me.'

'Not really,' she admitted. 'I told you, I've been living abroad. I've *heard* of you, of course, and Mrs Rogers told me one or two things, but I honestly don't know very much at all.'

He gave a rather strange smile. 'Good,' he said. 'For now, I'd like to keep it that way.' He glanced at his watch. 'We're well into the early hours of the morning. Are you still planning on running out on me?'

'No,' Rose said, with a resigned sigh. 'I think I'll have to stay, at least until the morning.'

'Then you'd better go back to bed and try to get some sleep. And don't worry,' he added, shooting a faintly mocking smile at her. 'I promise not to hit the bottle as soon as your back's turned.'

Rose wasn't altogether sure that a promise from this man meant anything. She was beginning to yawn hard now, though, and her eyes were getting very heavy, so she supposed she would just have to take his word. She couldn't sit here all night watching him, to make sure he didn't do anything stupid.

She got to her feet and trailed tiredly over to the door. 'Goodnight,' she said, stifling another yawn.

'See you in the morning,' said Nathan Hayward.

There was something in his tone that made Rose glance back at him; something that sent a very light shiver down her spine. He wasn't even looking at her, though, and she told herself she must have imagined it. All the same, she left the kitchen rather more hurriedly than she had meant to, and kept glancing nervously over her shoulder all the way up the stairs.

She slept much better than she had expected, and woke up feeling refreshed and relaxed. In fact, she was amazed that she had wanted to run away from Lyncombe Manor in the middle of the night.

'A lot of people get jittery after it gets dark,' she excused herself. 'And yesterday *was* a pretty traumatic day. No wonder you decided you'd had enough, and wanted out.'

She quickly washed and dressed, and then clattered downstairs. The suit of armour that had scared her so much last night didn't look in the least frightening in the bright light of day. And the manor itself looked as enchanting as always, lit this morning by great splashes of sunshine pouring through the lattice windows.

Rose decided that she needed a cup of coffee before she left, and so she made her way to the kitchen. When she opened the door, she found that Nathan was already there, cooking himself breakfast.

'Good heavens,' she said, 'you haven't been here all night, have you?'

'No, I managed a couple more hours of sleep—and without the help of alcohol,' he added.

'Do you mind if I make some coffee?'

'Help yourself. Do you want something to eat?'

'I'll just have a piece of toast,' replied Rose.

'No wonder you're so thin,' he remarked. 'Do you ever eat a decent meal?'

'All the time. But it doesn't matter how much I eat. I still stay skinny.'

Nathan expertly flipped a fried egg and some crisply fried rashers of bacon on to his plate. 'What are your plans for today?' he asked.

'I'd have thought that was fairly obvious. I'm going home. Well, not exactly home,' she amended. 'Home is where my family is, and that's Washington at the moment. My father was posted there earlier this year. But I'll be going back to Mrs Rogers' guest house— that's the nearest thing I've got to a home, at the moment.'

'You could stay here,' Nathan suggested casually.

Rose immediately stiffened. 'No, thank you,' she said at once.

'I wasn't suggesting that you move into my bed,' said Nathan with some amusement. 'I simply meant that you might want to take up that job you came after. And if you want to live in, to save money, that's no problem.'

But Rose could see that it could very easily become a *big* problem. Her bedroom was only a couple of doors away from Nathan's—and, although he hadn't shown any real interest in her, that didn't necessarily mean that she could rely on him to stay in his own room at night. And she didn't remember seeing any lock on her door.

'I don't think that would be a very good idea,' she said firmly.

He gave a faint smile. 'You don't trust me?'

'I think that I'd be very stupid if I did,' she retorted. 'Despite everything that's happened, I still hardly know you. No woman in her right mind would move in here in those circumstances.'

To her surprise, he didn't react angrily. Instead he merely nodded. 'You're probably right. But the east wing of the manor is virtually self-contained. It's got a bedroom, a small sitting-room and a bathroom. It even has its own entrance. The only room we'd have to share is the kitchen. You can use that wing, if you want to.'

Rose looked at him suspiciously. 'Why are you suddenly being so generous?'

'Perhaps I feel I owe it to you,' he said, after a moment's hesitation. Then he gave a faint smile. 'And I really do need a gardener. The card advertising the job has been in that shop for two weeks, and so far you're the only one who's shown any interest.' He seemed to sense that she was wavering, and he went on persuasively, 'If you like, you can take the job on a trial basis. Try it for a week. If, after a couple of days, you decide that you don't like the job—or me!—

you can pack it in, and I'll still pay you a full week's wages.'

It was a very tempting offer. Rose would be able to pay Mrs Rogers the money that she owed her, and she would also have a free roof over her head.

But the offer seemed just too good—and especially coming from Nathan Hayward, who had spent such a lot of time trying to get rid of her! Where was the catch?

'I don't know...' she muttered doubtfully.

He smiled at her, and she was nearly bowled over by the great blaze of charm that suddenly radiated from him. 'Of course you do,' he said smoothly. 'And it'll solve both our problems very neatly. You're short of money, and need somewhere to stay. I need a gardener pretty quickly, or the grounds of the manor are going to get completely out of hand.'

Rose wrinkled her nose indecisively. 'The east wing of the manor is really completely self-contained?' she said at last.

'You can even lock me out at night, if you want to,' he said, his slate-grey eyes reflecting his amusement.

She wasn't fooled by that light teasing, though. 'Will I need to do that?' she enquired in a challenging tone.

'I shouldn't think so,' he replied, the amusement fading from his face again now. 'You're just not my type. I can see that you've got a certain charm, with those big violet eyes and that mop of brown hair, but it really doesn't do a lot for me. And, as well as that, you're too innocent. I don't go for innocence. I prefer sophistication—and experience.'

Rose might have been thoroughly outraged by his declaration if it hadn't been for the distinctly world-weary tone of his voice. 'Perhaps you've had too much experience,' she found herself saying, much to her own surprise.

He looked at her strangely for a few moments. 'Maybe you're right,' he said a little shortly, at last. Then he gave a deep shrug, as if he had suddenly had more than enough of this conversation. 'Do you want the job, or not?' he asked directly.

'Yes,' said Rose. And a moment later, she wondered why she had said that. She knew instinctively that it wasn't a good idea to work for Nathan Hayward. And any female who agreed to live under the same roof as him definitely needed her brains tested!

She didn't change her mind about her sudden decision, though. Instead, she agreed to go and fetch her things after breakfast, and start work on the gardens of Lyncombe Manor that same afternoon.

This isn't a wise thing that you're doing, she warned herself. But then she looked again at Nathan Hayward; looked at his tired eyes and his too thin body, and she knew that he needed someone around right now. He had lived on his own for too long. It wasn't good for him to spend so much time alone.

Why did it have to be she who moved in, though? Perhaps because there was no one else around, she silently answered herself. No one else who cared. And did she care? Rose edged nervously away from that question. She didn't think she wanted to answer it at the moment. Or in the future, come to that.

She would do the job she was being paid to do, she decided. And she would be a friend to Nathan

Hayward—if a friend was what he needed. That was all, though. And she was definitely going to lock her door at night! She might feel sorry for him; there might be times when she almost liked him; but there was something in those slate-grey eyes of his that warned her not to trust him.

CHAPTER FOUR

MRS ROGERS looked rather shocked when Rose told her that she was moving into Lyncombe Manor.

'But Mr Hayward lives there all on his own, doesn't he?' she said.

'Yes, he does,' agreed Rose. 'But the rooms I'll be using are completely self-contained. And you did tell me that he was a nice man,' she added with a small grin.

Mrs Rogers' eyebrows drew together disapprovingly. 'Even the nicest of men can sometimes behave very badly. You can't really trust any of them. Men have urges that they can't always control,' she finished in a warning tone.

Rose had to fight hard to suppress her laughter. 'I'll be very careful,' she promised gravely.

Mrs Rogers sighed. 'Well, I suppose I can't stop you going. If you're only moving out because you're a little short of money, though, I want you to know that there's no need. You're welcome to stay on here, and pay me when you can.'

Rose was genuinely touched by her kind offer. 'Thanks, but I really think I'll be all right at Lyncombe Manor. If things don't work out, though, at least I'll know there's somewhere I can go.'

It didn't take her long to pack—she was travelling light—and half an hour later she was throwing her couple of bags into the back of the car.

She supposed the car was a luxury that she couldn't really afford, but she had hired it until the end of the month, and she very much doubted if she would get any refund if she returned it early. Anyway, she felt that she *needed* a car right now. Lyncombe Manor was right off the beaten track. No buses ran past the door, and the car would be her only means of escape if she ever had to leave in a hurry.

Not that the situation would arise, she assured herself firmly. She would work in the gardens during the day, and stay in her own rooms at night. She probably wouldn't see very much of Nathan Hayward at all.

She drove straight to Lyncombe Manor and, as she began to unload her bags from the car, she had the strange feeling that she was coming home. This house felt very familiar to her, as if she had already lived here for a long time instead of just spending a couple of nights here—and one of those had been spent locked in the cellar!

There was no sign of Nathan, but the front door was unlocked, so she picked up her bags and trudged inside.

The house felt deliciously cool after the blazing heat of the sun outside. She dumped her bags in the hall, and then stood there indecisively for a few moments. She didn't know where her rooms were, so she wasn't sure where to go from here.

'You'd better find Nathan,' she instructed herself. Where was he likely to be, though? It would take ages to search the entire house and grounds.

She wandered into the great hall, her soft-soled shoes making no sound on the stone-flagged floor. Then she stood quite still. There was no need to look for Nathan. He was here, slumped in the chair by the huge hearth, and very soundly asleep.

A lot of people looked more vulnerable when they were asleep, but Nathan Hayward merely looked relaxed. That in itself was something of a novelty, though. When he was awake, his lean body always seemed full of restless tension.

Rose moved a couple of steps nearer and studied him more closely. The line of his mouth wasn't so taut, and the creases between his dark brows had disappeared. It made him look surprisingly different— even younger.

How old *was* he? she wondered. It was very difficult to tell. Late twenties, early thirties, she supposed. She could probably find out, if she really wanted to. There had to be lots of newspaper clippings and features on him. It wouldn't be too hard to dig them out. They would give her some more background information on him, as well. So far, she knew extremely little. Mrs Rogers had told her a few basic facts, and Nathan himself had revealed next to nothing.

Did she *want* to know more? With a small start of surprise, Rose realised that she did. Not a good idea, she warned herself. Don't get too interested in this man. Although she couldn't have explained why, she instinctively knew that it would be dangerous.

At that moment, Nathan stirred, and then opened his eyes. For a brief instant, they looked blank and unfocused. Then, as they fixed on her face, a fleeting look of disappointment swept over them. 'Oh, it's you,' he muttered.

Rose had the distinct impression that he had wanted to see someone very different. That he hadn't *expected* to see this other person, but still hadn't quite given up hope that they would walk back into his life.

'Yes, it's me,' she agreed a little flatly.

'I suppose you want to see your rooms?' He levered himself stiffly to his feet. 'I'll take you up there.'

'How are the bruises?' she asked, as she followed him out of the great hall.

'Painful,' he replied briefly.

He didn't say anything else, and Rose got the message. He wasn't in a talkative mood. He led her up a narrow, winding flight of stairs at the far end of the house, and then opened the door at the top.

'This is the top floor of the east wing. It's got a bedroom, a bathroom, and another room at the end of the passage that you can use as a sitting-room, if you want to. No kitchen—you'll have to use the kitchen in the main wing of the house. That's the only room that we'll actually have to share, though.' Then he seemed to relax, and amusement briefly glimmered in his slate-grey eyes. 'The door to this wing has got quite a hefty lock on it. Just turn the key when you go to bed, and you should feel quite safe.'

'I already feel perfectly safe, thank you,' Rose replied, although not in the least truthfully. 'I'll unpack now, and start work after lunch.'

The amusement in his eyes grew more pronounced. 'You can wait until tomorrow, if you like. I'm not a particularly hard taskmaster.'

'I'd prefer to begin today,' she told him. 'I want to start earning my keep as soon as possible.'

Nathan shrugged. 'Do whatever you like. And feel free to use the kitchen facilities whenever you want to.'

'Perhaps you could tell me when you usually use them. Then we could draw up some kind of rota system, so that we're not always bumping into each other.'

His gaze rested on her speculatively. 'Are you trying to tell me that you want to avoid me as much as possible?'

'Of course not,' she said at once. 'But I thought that it was *you* who didn't want *me* around. I'm just trying not to get under your feet.'

'I'll tell you when I get tired of having you around,' he replied a little obliquely. 'And it's no use trying to draw up a rota. I eat—and sleep—at odd hours. I've never followed a set routine.'

'I suppose that's because you're a creative sort of person,' she said with a touch of humour. 'Do you get up in the middle of the night and write songs?'

Nathan's face changed. 'I don't write songs any more,' he said abruptly. And, before Rose had a chance to make any sort of reply, he swung round and strode out of the east wing.

Rose stared after him for a few moments. Then she gave a small grimace. 'Obviously the wrong thing to say,' she told herself wryly. 'Definitely a topic to be avoided in the future!'

She inspected the rooms that were to be her home for the foreseeable future, and found them to be more than adequate. The bedroom had another four-poster bed—they didn't seem to have any ordinary beds in Lyncombe Manor!—but this one was Victorian, with a lot of draperies and a hand-sewn patchwork quilt. A bow-fronted chest of drawers, a cavernous wardrobe and a couple of chairs completed the furnishing of the room.

The fittings in the bathroom looked fairly ancient, and the bath itself was free-standing with huge claw feet. When Rose turned on the taps, though, hot water instantly gushed out. She was relieved at that. She had the feeling that after a hard day's work in the overgrown gardens of Lyncombe Manor she was going to need a long soak in a hot bath to ease her tired muscles!

The last room was the sitting-room, which had a couple of elderly armchairs which were beginning to lose their stuffing, a fairly large table, bookcases which held rows of very serious-looking tomes, tall lamps with tasselled shades, and a small portable television which sat on top of an old bureau.

The best thing about the room was the view from the window. It looked out over the main gardens at the back of the house. Rose stood there for quite some while, imagining how the gardens would look after she had licked them into shape.

Eventually, she dragged herself away from the window and went to unpack. By the time she had finished, it was well past lunchtime, and she was starving.

She thought that Nathan would probably have eaten by now, so she went down to the kitchen with some confidence, certain that she would have it to herself. When she opened the door, though, she found him sitting at the table, and she gave a silent groan. He looked up as she came in, but didn't say anything.

'You seem to spend most of your time in this room,' she commented.

'It is my house,' he pointed out reasonably. 'I believe that entitles me to spend as much time as I like in whichever room I choose.'

She supposed he had a point there. 'I'll come back later and get something to eat, if that's more convenient,' she said, backing towards the door.

The beginnings of a smile touched the corners of his mouth. 'Are you running away from me again?'

'Of course not,' she said, a little crossly. 'It's just that I still haven't figured out what the rules are around here. I mean, am I meant to stay out of your way as much as possible? Or do you not mind my being around?'

'I've already told you, there aren't any rules in this house. Come and go as you please. Stay out of my way, if that's what you want, or hang around all the time. I don't care very much, either way.'

Rose decided that it wasn't much of a compliment, being told that he didn't care if she was there or not! On the other hand, she didn't really *expect* compliments from this man. And, on the whole, she thought she would probably feel happier—and a lot more relaxed—if she didn't spend too much time with him.

She still wanted something to eat, though. And she didn't think she could wait until Nathan decided to leave the kitchen and amble off to another part of the house. That could take all day! 'I'll make myself a couple of sandwiches,' she told him. 'If that's all right with you.'

He gave an impatient shrug of his shoulders. 'Stop asking me if things are all right! Just get on and do whatever you want to do. Have a sandwich, if you want one, or cook a whole damned dinner. The cupboards are full of food. Simply take what you want.'

Rose rummaged round, and quickly found what she needed. She shoved lettuce, tomatoes and ham between some slices of bread; then she grabbed a glass of fresh juice, and headed for the door.

'I think I'll eat this outside, in the sunshine,' she muttered. Then she hastily escaped from the kitchen.

Once she was out in the courtyard, she felt less edgy. As she sat in the sunshine, eating her lunch, she told herself that it was hardly surprising he was feeling rather moody at the moment. He was still stiff and bruised from his fall, which was bound to make his temper rather uncertain. On the other hand, Rose thought that he probably wasn't very even-tempered, even at the best of times!

When she had finished her lunch, she spent the rest of the afternoon wandering around the garden, making an increasingly long list of everything that needed to be done. She had found some paper and a pencil in the house, and she began to make a rough sketch of the grounds, noting down the positions of the flower-beds that she could see hidden under the grass and weeds, and discovering new features as she pushed her way through the overgrown wilderness. A fountain that didn't work, possibly because it was clogged up with water-weed; statues poking weathered heads out from behind shrubs that needed pruning; stone troughs full of small alpines that were nearly smothered by weeds.

By the end of her reconnaissance, she gave a long, deep sigh. There could be weeks of work here. Had she taken on more than she could handle?

No, she told herself with new firmness. She would start first thing in the morning, and she would work steadily on until she had licked this garden into shape. And although it would be hard work, she would enjoy it, because this house and its grounds somehow felt very special to her.

She ate dinner alone that evening—for once, there was no sign of Nathan anywhere near the kitchen—and then went up to her own rooms. For a while, she watched television. Then she sat at the window and watched dusk closing in over the gardens. She stayed there until it was too dark to see anything except the white roses gleaming with almost eerie paleness in the moonlight; then she went to bed in the big Victorian four-poster. She lay there for a while, listening to the sound of an owl hooting mournfully in the distance. Finally, she closed her eyes and slept soundly until the morning.

For the next few days, Rose worked harder than she had ever done in her life before. She discovered an old shed out at the back that housed an amazing variety of garden equipment, and she began by hauling out the largest of the three lawnmowers stored there. It was a huge old rotary mower, which took a lot of arm-wrenching yanks on the starter before it finally roared into life. It cut through the long swathes of grass like butter, though, and by the end of the day the main area of lawn had been cut and raked clear. Rose felt as if she had sweated off several pounds in the hot sunshine, and every muscle in her body ached, but she also felt a sense of triumph. A long soak in the claw-footed bath eased some of the soreness, and she fell asleep as soon as she tumbled into bed.

At the end of the first week, as she stood at her window breathing in the cool, sweet air of evening, she could see the considerable progress she had made. The outlines of the flower-beds were visible, all the grass was down to a reasonable length, and the largest of the weeds had been pulled up, giving the flowers some light and air. The following morning, she was going to tackle the fountain and the ornamental pond that surrounded it. It was choked with water-weed, which had to be cleared out if the water-lilies and other plants were to have a chance of survival.

After a while, she dragged herself away from the view and clambered into the bath. She soaked there for over half an hour until her overworked muscles felt more eased. Then she dried herself, and pulled on a thin cotton nightie. Instead of going directly to bed, she returned to the sitting-room for one more look at the garden in the moonlight.

It never failed to fascinate her, the way it changed under different lights. During the day, it was a warm and friendly place. At night, it became much more mysterious. She could almost imagine that she could see the ghosts of the people who had lived at Lyncombe Manor over the centuries, taking a stroll around the grounds under the safe cover of darkness.

When she *did* see something white move below, she almost jumped out of her skin. For a few moments, her pulse thumped wildly. Then she gave a shaky laugh of relief as she realised it was only Nathan, wearing a white sweatshirt.

She had seen very little of him during the past week. Sometimes, she had felt as if she were living at Lyncombe Manor on her own! It had never made her feel nervous, though, the sensation of being alone in this big old house. She felt so very comfortable and at home here. In fact, it was slightly alarming, the way she was beginning to love this place. What would happen when it was finally time for her to leave?

Rose decided that she didn't want to think about that. But she *did* want to see Nathan. There were a couple of things she needed to ask him. In fact, she had looked for him several times during the day, but hadn't been able to find him. Perhaps this would be a good time, before he disappeared again!

She slipped out of her nightdress, and pulled on jeans and a T-shirt. Then she hurried down the stairs that led out of the east wing, and made her way towards one of the doors that opened on to the courtyard.

As she headed through the gardens, towards the spot where she had seen Nathan, she began to wonder what he did with himself during the day—how he passed his time. He certainly didn't spend it watching her, to make sure she was doing her job properly. He had only put in an appearance a couple of times while she was working, to enquire briefly if she had everything she needed. In fact, the whole arrangement had worked out far better than she had ever expected. No hassles, no conflict, just two people living harmoniously in a house that was big enough to accommodate both of them more than comfortably.

She could see Nathan now. He was standing on the far side of the garden, by the large pond. The ducks which paddled round so energetically during the day had settled down for the night, and the water was very still and very bright, reflecting the pale light of the big moon overhead.

He didn't seem to hear her approaching, even though she wasn't making any particular effort to walk quietly. And when she touched him on the shoulder, he jumped visibly. As he swung round, there was enough moonlight for her to see that his eyes were glittering brightly.

'What the hell are you doing here?' he demanded, obviously not in the least pleased to see her.

'I wanted to talk to you.'

'Now? At this time of night?'

'It's barely eleven o'clock,' Rose pointed out reasonably. 'And you don't strike me as the sort of person who goes to bed very early.'

'There's not much point in going to bed when you don't sleep,' he muttered, the anger already fading from his voice.

'Well, I can't do much about your insomnia,' Rose said practically. 'But since you're still up, it gives me the chance to ask you a couple of things.'

Nathan didn't look as if he was at all interested in answering any of her questions, but Rose had learned to ignore his withdrawn moods by now. Instead, she just plunged on, certain that she would eventually get some kind of response out of him if she was persistent enough.

'I've finished most of the rough work in the garden,' she continued. 'I've got the grass down to a reasonable length and cleared most of the larger weeds. What I really want to know now is what kind of garden you actually want.'

His grey eyes came round to rest on her. 'A garden is a garden, isn't it?' he said in an indifferent tone.

'Of course not,' she replied a little impatiently. 'You can have a very formal garden, with the grass shaved right down, the plants set out in neat rows and absolutely everything in its place. Or you can go for a more informal effect, letting the roses ramble where they like, leaving the flowers in big clusters, and letting the daisies grow in the grass.'

'Do whatever you like,' he told her.

Rose looked at him a trifle disapprovingly. 'It's your house. You should be the one who chooses.'

Nathan's gaze became thoughtful. 'Which would *you* prefer?' Then, without giving her a chance to reply, he answered his own question. 'An informal garden, I should think.'

'How did you know that?' she asked curiously.

'Because you're a fairly informal type of person,' he replied in a dry voice. The moonlight was still bright enough to show her that his eyes had changed by now. His earlier indifference had disappeared without a trace, and his gaze was alert and unexpectedly intent. 'What else did you want to ask me?' he went on.

'Er—was there something else?' Rose asked in a rather squeaky voice.

'You said there were a couple of things,' he reminded her.

'Oh—yes—I think I did,' she muttered, wondering why on earth she suddenly felt so nervous. 'I've forgotten what the other thing was, though. Anyway, it's getting late. I'd better get off to bed. I'm planning on making an early start in the morning. I want to make the most of this good weather, before it breaks.'

She knew she was beginning to waffle, but she couldn't seem to stop. And she didn't know why she was gabbling on like this. She just knew that there had been a subtle change in the atmosphere between them and, for some reason, it was making her *very* edgy.

As she began to walk towards the house, Nathan fell into step beside her.

Rose stopped, and looked at him warily. 'I thought you wanted to stay outside for a while longer?'

'I didn't say that,' he replied easily.

'But—isn't a walk in the night air meant to be good for insomnia?'

'I've had a walk in the night air. It hasn't cured my insomnia, and I'm tired of walking round and round on my own.'

What was he saying? she wondered. That he wanted her to take a walk with him? Well, that was one invitation she wasn't taking up—not at this time of night!

Rose trotted on rather more briskly, hoping he would take the hint and go off in another direction. He easily kept pace with her, though, and seemed intent on following her right back into the house. Her pulse thumped a little harder. I'm *not* nervous, she told herself staunchly. I *can* cope with this man.

They had reached the courtyard now, and Rose stopped again. In the moonlight, it looked impossibly romantic, with the tubs of ferns casting faint, fronded shadows in the silver light, while the darker mass of the house rose round them on three sides.

'Why did you buy this place?' she asked him suddenly.

She had no idea why she had asked him such a question, but she was suddenly very curious to hear his answer.

Nathan gave a brief shrug. 'I told the estate agent that I was looking for a secluded property in its own grounds, and this was the first suitable place that he came up with.'

'But even if he'd sent you a dozen suitable properties, this would have been the one that you finally chose, wouldn't it?' she persisted. 'I mean, it's so absolutely perfect.'

'Actually, I bought it without seeing it.' When she gazed at him incredulously, he gave another shrug. 'I was abroad at the time. I couldn't fly back and inspect every house that looked as if it might fit my requirements. This one seemed to have everything I needed, so I said I'd take it.'

'You must be every estate agent's idea of the ideal customer!' she said drily.

She glanced up at him as she spoke, and she found that he was looking at her with that rather intent expression again.

'What is it?' she asked a little uneasily.

'I'm just beginning to realise how much you fit in with this place,' he said slowly.

'What do you mean by that?'

'You look as if you belong here. As if you've always been here.'

'I *feel* as if I belong here,' she admitted in a low voice. 'Although that's silly, because I only moved in a few days ago, and I probably won't be staying for very long.'

'Maybe. Maybe not,' Nathan said, rather cryptically.

Rose was about to ask him what he meant by that, but then decided that she would rather not know. There was something about this place at night that made conversation far easier than it was during the day. And she had the feeling that it could all too easily become an *intimate* conversation. Of course, all this moonlight didn't help. The pale silver glow that lit everything could have a very unsettling effect on the senses. She was already aware that she was becoming uncomfortably receptive to Nathan's changes of mood. She just hoped that he wasn't finding it equally easy to read her own thoughts and feelings.

She tried to say that she was going straight into the house now, but she couldn't quite seem to get the words out. Nathan wasn't helping, either. He kept looking and *looking* at her, as if he was really seeing her for the very first time.

'I wish you wouldn't keep staring like that,' she said at last, annoyance helping her to find her tongue. 'It's very——'

'Very what?' he prompted softly.

She had been about to say 'unsettling', but changed her mind at the last moment. 'Rude!' she muttered instead.

'I've never pretended to be particularly polite,' he said in a lazy voice.

He sounded far more relaxed than usual, and in a totally different mood from the one he had been in when she had first approached him this evening. And that had been a mistake! she decided with a grimace. She should have stayed in her own room, and talked to him in the morning.

'I just don't know why you keep staring at me,' she said, a little irritably.

'Perhaps it's because you look different tonight,' Nathan replied after a short pause. 'And I can't quite figure out why.'

'Everyone looks different at night. It's a trick of the light. I'll look my usual boring self in the morning.'

'Maybe. But right at this moment, you don't look boring at all.'

His tone had become silkier, which should perhaps have warned her. Stupidly, though, she let her curiosity get the better of her.

'If I don't look boring, how do I look?' she couldn't help asking.

Nathan gave an odd smile. 'Like no one I've ever been involved with before.'

'Is that a compliment?'

'No,' he replied calmly. 'Just a statement. I don't go in for compliments.'

'Then what *do* you go in for?'

His slate-grey eyes seemed to turn almost silver as they reflected the light of the moon. 'Right now—this,' he said smoothly.

Afterwards, Rose realised that she had really been incredibly naïve. She should never have asked that last question. It had just given him the opening he had been looking for. She genuinely hadn't expected to find herself in this sort of situation, though. After all, hadn't he told her earlier in the week that he wasn't interested in her? That she wasn't his type?

Well, for someone who wasn't his type, she was certainly now being very thoroughly kissed!

His mouth was warm and hard, and unexpectedly demanding. This wasn't a friendly sort of kiss. Or the sort of kiss given by someone who was only marginally interested, and just making the most of an advantageous situation.

This was the sort of kiss given by a man who had suddenly decided that he had been without female company for far too long. A man who wanted much more than she was prepared to give! When she tried to tell him that his kisses weren't in the least welcome, though, she didn't get very far. His lips easily stifled the words she was struggling to get out, and she had the feeling that he was quite deliberately preventing her from saying anything.

She was flushed and hot by the time she finally managed to wrench her mouth free for a few moments.

'What do you think you're doing?' she muttered at him.

Nathan lifted one dark eyebrow. 'I'd have thought that was perfectly obvious.'

'I do not want to be kissed!' she told him furiously. 'And especially not by you.'

'Why not?' he asked calmly. 'I'm quite proficient at it. Didn't you enjoy it?'

'That is not the point!' she almost howled.

'I should think it's very much the point. At least, it always is as far as I'm concerned. Do you ever kiss for any other reason except for pleasure?'

He was trying to side-track her, and Rose was determined she wasn't going to let that happen. A few moments later, though, the entire conversation became irrelevant as he moved forward in one supple movement, and kissed her for the second time.

She had thought that the first kiss was fairly devastating, but this one brought a definite tremble to her knees. And it wasn't just his mouth at work this time, endlessly moving on hers in a determined effort to force it into submission. His *hands* had joined in the assault—although Rose had the feeling that 'assault' didn't quite describe what was happening to her.

Without the slightest hesitation, he headed his hands straight for her breasts. Rose winced slightly, and waited for him to show obvious signs of disappointment. Her breasts were very small—they always had been. Most of the men in her life—and, admittedly, there hadn't been very many—had skimmed over them fairly quickly, with little more than a perfunctory caress.

Nathan's hands stayed exactly where they were, though. It was such a novel sensation that Rose forgot to try and pull away. His fingertips lightly rubbed the little peaks into an unexpected hard tightness, which pushed eagerly against the thin cotton of her T-shirt, as if aching for more of this new attention. Then his palms cupped the slight swell underneath and, to Rose's amazement, he didn't seem to *care* that she lacked the heavy fullness that she sometimes—in fact, quite often—envied in other women.

Another kiss was being inflicted on her now—and she was horrified to find that her inclination to protest was growing fainter and fainter.

Don't get carried away, she warned herself with a quick surge of alarm. None of this means anything—and especially not to Nathan Hayward. *You* don't mean anything to him. You're here, and you're female, and he's beginning to think you're available. That's as far as it goes. As far as it'll ever go.

When he released her mouth this time, needing air as much as she did, she was ready for him. One quick movement freed her from the touch of his hands, and two steps backwards put her out of the range of his dangerously expert mouth.

'I thought I wasn't your type,' she reminded him in a voice that came out far more breathlessly than she had expected.

'I thought that, too,' he agreed. His voice was soft, but there was something in the undertone that warned her she wasn't out of danger yet.

'You like women who are sophisticated. Experienced.' As she flung his own words back at him, she was surprised to find herself feeling slightly bitter that she was never going to fit into either of those categories.

'Right now, I want someone who isn't cool. Isn't blonde,' he said, his gaze very bright.

She remembered that he had told her once before that he was glad she wasn't a blonde. Her brief surge of anger began to drain away. Instead, she found herself looking at his mouth, which had set into a strange twist. And his eyes had become curiously distant.

'Are you all right?' she found herself asking, at last.

'Yes, I'm all right,' he said, after a long pause. 'I think that, finally, I really am all right. It was hardly fair to use you, just to prove that to myself, though.'

Rose shook her head a little impatiently. 'I haven't the faintest idea what you're talking about.'

'Of course you haven't.' He gave an odd smile. 'Perhaps you'd better go on up to bed. I think we've both had more than enough for tonight.'

With that, he turned his back on her and walked away. Rose stared after him, full of questions that she just didn't have the nerve to ask. What had *that* all been about?

She realised that her body had begun to shake gently with reaction. The night had held too many surprises, and she still felt as if she was in a faint state of shock. First, those kisses—and fairly unforgettable kisses they had been! Then the touch of his hands, awakening sensations that were virtually brand-new to her. And, finally, those puzzling remarks and his abrupt exit.

She stood in the centre of the moonlit courtyard for a couple more minutes. Then she very slowly walked back to her room. Of course, she hadn't *wanted* things to go any further, she told herself more than once. After all, she was the one who had put a stop to the whole thing—wasn't she?

Or had Nathan simply run out of interest in her? For some reason, she didn't like that idea, and she quickly pushed it out of her head.

Rose reached the door to the east wing, went through it, closed it behind her, and then hesitated for several seconds before finally locking it. Why bother? she asked herself. He won't be coming up here tonight.

And it was a little alarming how disappointed she was by that thought.

CHAPTER FIVE

ROSE didn't go to bed straight away. She felt too disturbed by the unexpected events of the night. She needed to sort out how she felt about this sudden change in their relationship before there was any chance of her getting to sleep.

She certainly knew how she *ought* to feel. Thoroughly outraged that he had jumped on her like that, and determined to leave Lyncombe Manor first thing in the morning. After all, what had happened once could very easily happen again.

Yet that prospect didn't frighten her half as much as it should have. Whatever else she felt about Nathan Hayward—and heaven knew, she seemed to have a whole jumble of feelings about him right now—he didn't scare her. Which was odd, really, considering that there were only the two of them in the house. A situation like this ought to make her feel extremely jumpy.

Rose wandered into the bedroom, and slowly stripped off her jeans and T-shirt. Her nightdress was lying on the bed, where she had tossed it earlier. Instead of putting it on, though, she turned to face the full-length mirror on the far side of the room.

She had never been very impressed by the sight of her naked body, and rarely bothered to look at it in any detail. She was a tall, angular girl, with small breasts, a narrow waist, a flat stomach and thin hips. Probably her legs were her best feature. They were long and graceful. 'Legs like a racehorse' her father used to say.

Rose sniffed. Being compared to a racehorse really wasn't very flattering. She would much rather be well-rounded and voluptuous!

With a small sigh, she pulled on her nightie. She decided she would have to think about this new situation again in the morning. Obviously, there were decisions to be made, but she just didn't feel up to it right now. Perhaps after a long sleep, her head would feel clearer; she would be less confused by the memory of Nathan's hands moving with exquisite purposefulness over her body.

Although she hadn't actually expected to, she slept surprisingly well. And she woke up with a quite different attitude towards what had happened last night. It wasn't the touch of his hands that she remembered. It was the fact that he had had the nerve to try anything so intimate in the first place!

With rising indignation, she recalled the demanding fierceness of his kisses, and the way he had calmly assumed that he had the *right* to behave like that. Just because he had felt a passing twinge of desire, or lust, or whatever it had been, she had been expected to go along with it, to be as responsive as he had required her to be. She felt as if she had stopped being a person, and had become just a female body he had seized hold of to try and satisfy his sudden needs.

Rose knew perfectly well that she was being a little unreasonable, that it hadn't been *quite* like that. She had worked herself up into a state of self-righteous anger by now, though, and she wasn't ready to let go of it just yet.

She quickly washed and dressed, then she marched downstairs. Her anger deflated a little when she discovered that Nathan wasn't in the kitchen or the great hall. Then it puffed up again as she realised that he might be hiding from her.

He knew that he had been in the wrong last night, she told herself fiercely. And he didn't want to come face to face with her in case she forced him to admit it.

If she had been in a calmer mood, it might have occurred to her that it was highly unlikely that Nathan was afraid to face anyone, let alone a twenty-three-year-old girl. She was bristling with indignation by this time, though. And she was determined to find him, and confront him.

There were several more rooms on the ground floor of Lyncombe Manor, and she set out to look in every one of them. If he wasn't there, she would scour the top floor of the house, and then thoroughly search the grounds.

As it turned out, very little searching was necessary. A narrow passage led her to a room at the back of the house and, as she neared it, she could hear the sound of someone playing the piano in a rather desultory manner.

Rose pushed the door open and found herself in a room that she hadn't been in before. The windows were opened on to the gardens, and scented air drifted in, mixing with the distinct smell of alcohol that permeated the room.

The piano was situated in the far corner of the room. Nathan was sitting behind it, his hands idle on the keys now, and his gaze resting on her as she walked further into the room.

'Surely you haven't begun to drink this early in the morning?' she said with some disgust, noticing the nearly empty bottle in front of him.

'No, I haven't,' he replied in that unruffled tone that he sometimes used when he wasn't quite sober. 'I began last night. Soon after we parted, in fact.'

'Well, if you've been drinking for that long, then it's no wonder that you're sitting down,' Rose remarked in a totally disapproving voice. 'If you try to stand up, you'll probably fall over.'

'I never fall over,' Nathan stated calmly. 'As a matter of fact, I never get drunk, no matter how long or how much I drink. It blurs the world a little round the edges, though, and sometimes that's exactly what I need.'

Rose realised that she was getting side-tracked. She hadn't come here to discuss his drinking habits.

'I think you know exactly why I'm here,' she said bluntly.

'Of course,' agreed Nathan. 'You've come to lecture me about last night.'

'You're right about that!'

'What do you want me to say about it? That I'm sorry?' He gave a small shrug. 'But I'm not. It was just something that I felt like doing, and so I did it.'

Rose glared at him. 'And because you felt like it, that made it all right? No matter how *I* felt about it?'

His eyes met and held hers. 'I got the impression that you didn't mind too much.'

'How would you know?' she demanded hotly. 'Did you stop to ask? Did you even care?'

He slid his fingers slowly through the dark, tousled strands of his hair, as if he didn't really want to carry on with this conversation any longer.

'I didn't ask because I didn't need to,' he said at last. 'I know when a woman is—or isn't—enjoying it, when I kiss her. And did I care?' His shoulders moved briefly in an uncharacteristically uncertain gesture. 'I suppose I must have, or I wouldn't have kissed you in the first place.'

Rose was finding it infuriatingly hard to remain angry with him. She tried to stoke up her indignation again, but it was very difficult now that she was actually face to face with him. She always seemed to see things in a rather different light when she was this close to him.

She walked over to the open windows, and stared out at the gardens. There was still a lot of work to be done, but she could see the curved outlines of the lawns and flower-beds now, the glint of water from the pond, and the great splashes of colour from the flowers that had been liberated from the choking clumps of weed.

Finally, she turned back to face Nathan again. She realised that he had hardly taken his eyes off her since she had walked into the room, and yet it didn't make her feel uncomfortable any longer. In fact, she rather liked it when he looked at her.

'What are you going to do now?' asked Nathan at length. 'Pack your bags and leave?'

'If I had any sense, I suppose that's what I'd do,' she said slowly. She let her own gaze drift over to meet his. 'What did you mean last night, when you said that you wanted someone who wasn't cool and wasn't blonde?'

'I think you know perfectly well what I meant,' he replied, after a short pause.

And because Rose had had plenty of time to think about it, she was sure that she did. Jancis Kendall—the girl who had sung his songs, who had been the other half of their hugely successful singer/song-writer partnership. She was a blonde.

Rose gave a soft sigh. What was she getting into here? Something deep and complicated, that much was certain. And was it something that she would be able to get out of again easily, if she wanted to?

She stared out at the gardens again. They seemed particularly tranquil this morning, basking in the hot sunshine that blazed down from the clear blue sky. Birds sung cheerfully in the nearby trees, the ducks quacked more raucously from time to time, and there was the soft hum of bees as they hovered around the roses that climbed all over the walls of the manor.

'Do you *want* me to stay?' she asked at last, keeping her back to him.

'A few days ago, I'd probably have told you that I didn't care one way or the other. But I'm beginning to realise that you've brought a little sanity back into my life. I don't know quite how you've done it, but I think I'd like to hold on to it for a while longer.'

At that, Rose finally turned round and looked at him. 'Would you be saying all this if you were completely sober?' she asked bluntly.

'Probably not. Does the fact that I'm slightly drunk make any difference?'

She didn't know. But she did know that it might be a very long time before she found him willing to talk like this again. If there was anything she wanted to know—and when she thought about it, there were quite a lot of things—this was the time to ask him.

'If I'm going to stay, then I want to know a lot more about you,' she told him. 'Up until last night, it didn't really matter, because there wasn't much contact between us. Things seem to be changing, though, so I think it's time you filled me in on some of the details.'

'What do you want?' he asked with the first glimmerings of a dry smile. 'My life story? It isn't very interesting.'

'That's hard to believe! You've done so much, written all those gorgeous songs, travelled just about everywhere. You were famous. Well, you still *are* famous. Your songs are played all over the world. Why did you stop writing them?' she asked curiously.

'There didn't seem much point after Jancis and I split up,' Nathan said in a flat tone.

It was the first time she had ever heard him say her name. In fact, she had the feeling that it was a very long time since he had actually said it out loud. His voice had seemed to linger over that one word, as if he was carefully testing his own reaction to it.

Rose thought that it might not be a good idea to ask him straight out about Jancis Kendall. He might just clam up again, and she would never be able to find out anything. Instead, she decided to lead up to it gently.

'How did you get started as a songwriter?' she asked. 'It must be difficult to get a career like that off the ground.'

'I guess I was lucky,' said Nathan. 'I used to write all the material for a local group in my home town. They sent a demo disc to a record company, and ended up with a recording contract. They had good management and good publicity, and they eventually made the charts. Other groups and singers liked the stuff I wrote for them, got in touch, and asked if I'd write something for them. For a couple of years, I had almost more work than I could handle. Then I met Jancis.'

He seemed to find it easier to say her name this time. Even so, he hesitated for a couple of moments before going on.

'She had a good voice, deep and wide-ranging. And, just as important, she knew exactly how to put over a song. She hadn't yet made the big time, but she was already a professional to her fingertips. I knew that, with the right material and careful handling, she could go all the way to the top.'

'She certainly managed that, all right,' agreed Rose. 'At the height of her career, she must have been one of the best-known singers around. The two of you were an ideal team. You might have been made for each other.'

'Oh, we were,' agreed Nathan cynically. 'At least, I certainly fitted all *her* requirements. I wrote her songs, I was always at her beck and call, and I kept her warm in bed at night—when she required it.'

With an effort, Rose succeeded in keeping her face fairly expressionless.

Nathan lightly raised one eyebrow. 'You don't look particularly shocked.'

'Why should I be?' she replied, somehow managing to keep her voice fairly steady. 'I never imagined, for one moment, that you had a strictly platonic relationship.'

'No,' he confirmed softly, 'it certainly wasn't platonic. But it was fairly one-sided.'

He poured himself out another drink and quickly swallowed it. Rose had enough sense not to try and stop him. Anyway, if he began to sober up, he might stop talking, and she suddenly felt a strong need to know exactly what had happened between Nathan and Jancis Kendall.

'One-sided on your side, or on hers?' she asked in a low tone.

'Oh, I was the one who was obsessed,' Nathan said rather harshly. 'I was the one who came when she called, stayed away when she didn't want me, and arranged my life so that it fitted in with hers. She was always cool, always in control of everything. I grew to hate that, when I was so *out* of control.'

Rose stared at him in growing amazement. 'I can't imagine you behaving like that,' she said at last.

'No one can, until it happens to them. I certainly didn't think I could ever be so dependent on such a twisted relationship,' he said with some bitterness. 'And she knew exactly how to keep my obsession going. If it looked as if I was getting so frustrated that I was likely to explode or walk out, then she would invite me back into her bed for a while. I don't think she particularly enjoyed sleeping with me. In fact, I don't think she actually liked sex very much. But in a way, that just turned it into more of a challenge. I kept trying harder and harder to *make* her like it. I always thought that, next time, I'd finally get that response I was looking for. Next time, it would be as good for her as it was for me.'

He took another drink, as if he needed the strong alcohol to dull the memories. Rose bit her lip. When she had come looking for him this morning, she hadn't expected to hear anything like this. It was so personal, so private. He was allowing her to share the darker side of his life, his failures and his most intimate memories—and she didn't know why.

'How long did all this go on?' she asked at last, in a very subdued voice.

'From the day we met until the day that we finally split up,' he answered in a taut voice. 'Nearly two years in all. Most obsessive relationships burn themselves out in a few months. Mine burned deeper than most, so I suppose that's why it took longer.'

'Who was the one who finally walked away from it?' asked Rose. She didn't know why, but it seemed very important for her to know. 'You? Or Jancis?'

'I was the one who walked away. Although, by then, she was quite happy to let me go. She didn't try to stop me. Her career had hit new heights—she didn't think she needed me any more. There were other good songwriters around. As far as she was concerned, I had become replaceable.'

'Where did you go? What did you do?'

'What did I do?' Nathan repeated. 'I didn't need to do anything. I had more than enough money to live on, and the royalties from my songs kept pouring in. Where did I go? Abroad, for quite a while. Several months, in fact. I kept travelling around—I couldn't seem to settle anywhere. Then I got tired of living out of a suitcase, and decided to come home. I wanted to live somewhere secluded, though. Somewhere Jancis couldn't find me—if she ever decided that she wanted to. The estate agents finally found me this place.'

'I suppose you felt safe here from reporters, as well,' Rose said slowly. 'They must have hounded you, after the break-up. Even in America, there were a lot of

Romance Readers

take 4 Temptations plus a cuddly teddy
and surprise mystery gift

◆ Absolutely Free! ▶

We're inviting you to discover why the Temptation
series has become so popular with romance readers.

A tempting FREE offer from Mills & Boon

We'd love you to become a regular reader of
Temptation and discover the modern sensuous
love stories that have made it one of our most
popular series. To welcome you we'd like you to
have 4 Temptation books, a Cuddly Teddy and
a Mystery Gift ABSOLUTELY FREE.

Then, each month you could look forward to
receiving 4 Brand New Temptations,
delivered to your door, postage & packing
FREE! Plus our free Newsletter full of author
news, competitions and special offers.

**Turn the page for
details of how to
claim your free gifts!**

Reader Service
FREEPOST
P.O. Box 236
Croydon
Surrey CR9 9EL

Send NO money now

FREE Books Coupon

Yes Please rush me my 4 FREE TEMPTATIONS & 2 FREE GIFTS! Please also reserve me a Reader Service Subscription. If I decide to subscribe, I can look forward to receiving 4 brand New Temptations, each month, for just £5.80, post and packing FREE. If I decide not to subscribe I shall write to you within 10 days. I can cancel or suspend my subscription at any time. I can keep the books and gifts whatever I decide. I am over 18 years of age.

9A0T

FREE

FREE

Mrs/Miss/Mr _____

Address _____

_____

_____ Postcode _____

Signature _____

stories in the Press. I didn't read them, but I remember seeing them.'

'I was the one who walked away, but Jancis told everyone that she was the one who decided to break up the partnership. She told the Press a lot of other things, as well. She hinted at money problems, even fraud. She gave the gutter Press a lot of behind-the-scenes details that should have stayed private. And what the Press didn't actually get out of her, they made up for themselves. For a cool lady, she certainly enjoys publicity and being the very centre of attention,' he finished tightly.

'What happened to her after you split up?' asked Rose. 'I mean, I know she's still around, but I don't know how she's doing. I'm afraid I'm not very up on the current music scene,' she said a little apologetically.

'Her career's on the slide,' Nathan said shortly. 'The blaze of publicity after our break-up kept things going for her for a while, but she hasn't been able to find new material that suits her style of singing. Good songwriters aren't as common as she supposed,' he said with grim satisfaction.

'Is that why you're still hiding away down here?' Rose said perceptively. 'You think she'll reach a point where she wants you back?'

'She won't want *me*. But she'll want my songs—and she'll do whatever she has to do to make sure she gets them.'

'You're afraid she'll try to start the affair up all over again? That she'll call you up, and you'll go running back to her, the way you always did?'

Nathan's slate-grey eyes took on a new brilliance. 'I'm never running back to that bitch again! I'm free of her now. It's taken me a hell of a long time, but I've finally got her out of my system.'

Rose's gaze rested uneasily on the almost empty bottle standing in front of him, on the piano. 'It's very easy to exchange one addiction for another,' she said hesitantly.

For the first time, the glimmerings of a smile touched the taut corners of his mouth. 'You think I'm turning into an alcoholic? That it's the bottle that I can't leave alone now, instead of Jancis?'

'You do seem to drink a lot,' she told him, not quite sure where she was finding the courage to talk to him like this.

'Occasionally, I drink a lot,' he corrected her. 'But I often go for weeks now without even touching the stuff. And I'm not an alcoholic. I'd know if I were— and admit it. Hell,' he went on tiredly, 'if I can admit to my addictive obsession with Jancis Kendall, then admitting to alcoholism would be child's play.'

Rose moved a little nearer, so that she could see his face more clearly. 'Why did you tell me about Jancis?' she asked curiously.

'I don't know,' Nathan said with unexpected frankness. 'When you first turned up here, I thought you were just a nuisance. Then I gradually began to get used to having you around. And last night...'

'What about last night?' Rose said uncertainly, as his voice trailed away.

He gave a small shrug. 'I'd told myself that I wasn't interested in you. That you weren't my type. And that was the truth. Now—I'm not so sure.' His faint smile suddenly turned into a full grin. 'Want to stick around, to find out how all of this turns out?' he challenged her, his gaze catching and holding hers.

'I don't know.' Rose moved away from him again, unexpectedly disturbed by this entire conversation. She had never thought, for one moment, that things would go in this direction. And she wasn't at all sure that she could deal with the situation.

'Do you know how long it is since I've touched a piano?' Nathan said, changing the subject.

'No,' she said.

'Not for nearly eighteen months—not since my split with Jancis. This morning, though, I've been picking out tunes. Nothing spectacular, but they're the first ideas I've had for songs for a very long time.'

'And you think that's something to do with me?' she asked warily.

'I've no idea.' He looked up at her. 'What do you think?'

Rose thought that she had had about as much of this as she could cope with at the moment. There were a lot of things that she needed to mull over, and she wanted to do it well away from this man, who seemed so very good at springing surprises on her.

'I think that I've got a lot of work to be getting on with. I also think that I might still want to leave,' she added honestly. 'I'm not at all sure that I want to be a cure for all your problems.'

The smile he gave her this time was a very confident one. 'I don't think you'll walk out on me, Rose. Not yet.'

And the really disturbing thing was that she had the feeling that he was right.

Rose spent what was left of the morning in the garden, hacking away at the water-weed that was choking the fountain and the ornamental pond that surrounded it. The sun was bright and scorching, and she was soon very hot, sweaty and tired.

She had come out here into the fresh air because she had needed to get away from Nathan for a while, and also because she had wanted time to think over all the things that, amazingly, he had told her about his relationship with Jancis Kendall.

She had to admit that she hadn't enjoyed listening to all the details. She didn't *want* to know that he had been obsessed with Jancis. And then there were all the details that he hadn't told her, but she could too easily imagine for herself. The rows, the accusations, the fraught scenes—and Nathan and Jancis in bed together, him full of a heated need, while she allowed him to do whatever he pleased, without ever giving anything of herself back to him.

Rose shivered violently, despite the humid heat that surrounded her. Stop thinking about it! she ordered herself sharply. It's over—he said it was over.

But she didn't see how a relationship like that could ever be completely over. The memories would be too vivid, the uncontrollable intensity of feeling would surely always haunt you. And any other kind of relationship must seem dull and insignificant in comparison.

She hauled the last tangle of weeds from the pond, and dumped them in the wheelbarrow. Then she straightened up and rubbed her stiff back. Her jeans and T-shirt were muddy and dirty, and her skin was damp with sweat after her exertions. It hadn't been necessary to tackle the job with such vigour, but Rose had felt the need to work off some of the turmoil that was churning round inside of her.

She turned round, ready to trudge back to the house for a bath before lunch. Then she saw Nathan standing in the courtyard, almost as if he was waiting for her.

Rose didn't hesitate. She shot off in the opposite direction, disappearing from sight in just seconds. She had no idea why she had suddenly felt she couldn't face him. Nor did she have any idea where she was going.

She was almost at the boundary of the grounds to the manor now. There were no fences, only a stretch of shady woodland that covered the central part of the valley.

A clearly discernible path led through the woodland. After only a moment's hesitation, Rose followed it. The trees sheltered her overheated skin from the sun, and the silence of the wood was soothing. The only sounds she could hear were a jumble of different bird songs, and the gentle hum of insects.

The path wound on for quite a way; then the trees thinned out and she could see the rest of the valley stretching ahead of her. Sheep grazed on the steep hillsides, and a small river ran along the floor of the valley. The path followed the river, which glittered in the sunshine that was beating down on Rose's head again now.

She hardly noticed the blazing brightness of the sun. Instead, she just kept walking. After a quarter of an hour, she reached the end of the valley, and discovered that it opened out into a small cove. She had reached the sea.

Rose hadn't realised that Lyncombe Manor was this near to the coast. The cove was sheltered on both sides by outcrops of rock, which made it completely private, and the sea looked incredibly cool and inviting. Without hesitation, she walked towards it, pausing only to strip off her sweaty, mud-stained clothes at the water's edge. Finally, wearing just a tiny pair of cotton pants, she stepped into the water.

She gave a small yelp as its coldness hit her hot skin. Then she plunged on, savouring the sharp contrast in temperature. After a while, it became too deep for her to wade any further, and she began to swim.

Since she wasn't feeling particularly energetic after her exertions of the morning, followed by the long walk, she swam fairly slowly. Then, after a while, she flipped over on to her back and just floated.

At last, feeling refreshed—and much cleaner—she headed back towards the small patch of beach. She was just about to leave the water and retrieve her clothes, when she saw Nathan walking down to the cove.

'Oh, no,' she groaned, and quickly backed out into deeper water again. With a bit of luck, he wouldn't even see her.

Nathan's gaze was already fixed on her, however, even though he was still some distance away. He sauntered down to the beach, and the only time he looked away from her was when his eyes moved thoughtfully to her pile of clothes sitting at the water's edge.

'You don't seem to have brought a towel with you,' he commented at last.

Rose scowled at him as she bobbed up and down in the chilly water. 'I didn't bring a swimming costume, either.'

He began to look much more interested. 'How are you planning to get dry? Of course, you could always run around naked in the hot sun,' he suggested.

'While you stand there and watch me?' she shot back indignantly.

Nathan gave one of his infrequent smiles. 'You don't strike me as a particularly shy girl.'

'I'm not an exhibitionist, either!' Rose was beginning to get distinctly cold and extremely irritable. 'Would you mind going away? Or at least turning your back?'

'I think I'd rather stay here and watch. I rather like watching you, Rose.'

She gazed at him warily. 'What exactly do you mean by that?'

'Quite often, I sit and watch you working in the garden. You move well—did you know that? For a tall girl, you're very graceful.'

For some reason, the thought of him sitting in the shadowed rooms of the house, watching her, made her feel more than a little uneasy. Then Rose shook her head. That wasn't a problem right now. It was getting out of the water and safely back into her clothes that was the problem!

Goose-pimples were beginning to run over her skin. Suddenly fed up with the entire situation, she lifted her head defiantly. She had had enough of this! She tossed back her wet hair, and began to wade towards the beach.

To begin with, she held her hands in front of her bare breasts. Then she gave a small grimace. What was the point of trying to hide behind her hands? There wasn't that much to cover!

She let her arms fall back to her sides, straightened her shoulders, and marched up the beach. When she reached her pile of clothes, she sat down beside them. She couldn't pull them back on while she was still wet. She would have to sit in the sun for a few minutes, until her skin had dried off.

Nathan sat down beside her. Strangely enough, she didn't feel nearly as embarrassed as she had thought she would, even though he was still looking at her. For some reason, he made her feel comfortable with her own body, which was something that no other man had ever managed before.

'You're good to look at,' he remarked at last. 'And not an ounce of spare fat in sight.'

'Thin, you mean,' said Rose, pulling a face. 'My father's always telling me I look like a racehorse. Long-legged and lanky.'

'There's nothing wrong with being thin.'

'A lot of men think so,' she replied in a defensive tone. He was beginning to hit a rather raw nerve.

He looked at her a little sharply. 'One man in particular?'

His instant perceptiveness surprised her. 'Well—as a matter of fact, yes,' she admitted with some reluctance.

'Someone special?'

'I thought for a while that he might be.'

'Where did you meet him? Back in America?'

'He was attached to the embassy,' said Rose. 'We had a good thing going, and we began to get really close.'

Nathan frowned, as if he didn't like hearing about her relationships with other men. 'What went wrong?' he asked rather shortly.

'I didn't quite fit his picture of the ideal woman. He didn't like me the way I was.'

'What did he want you to do about it?'

'He wanted me to have cosmetic surgery to enlarge my breasts. Silicon implants!' Rose gave a snort of disgust. 'As if that would somehow make me more female!'

Nathan growled something under his breath, and it seemed to be a very explicit comment on the subject.

She looked at him a little anxiously. 'You don't think I was wrong to refuse, do you?'

'I think that anyone who wants to change one inch of you is completely insane,' he stated flatly.

She hadn't expected him to say anything quite like that. Then she looked down at herself rather ruefully. 'You have to admit that there isn't very much of me.'

'Small can still be beautiful,' Nathan said, in a tone that was beginning to change in timbre. 'And you're a lovely shape.'

A little heat was beginning to creep into Rose's face now—and it had nothing to do with the sunshine beating down on her skin.

'This conversation is starting to get very personal,' she said, with a faintly embarrassed laugh.

'There's nothing wrong with being personal,' replied Nathan. His voice had changed still further, and his eyes seemed to have become overbright. 'And I'd certainly like to stay on the subject of your breasts a little longer.' His hand moved towards her as he spoke, and by the time his voice had faded away his palm had gently cupped the slight underswell. 'Nice,' he murmured. 'I like touching you, as well as watching you.'

And Rose liked being touched. His fingers were warm and sure, moving over her with confidence, as if they knew exactly what they were about.

She gave a brief, involuntary sigh as his fingertips lingered lightly over the small, tight, pink peaks. He heard it, and seemed pleased by her response. Then he bent his head, so that the moistness of his tongue licked gently over the same path.

Rose felt his dark, tousled hair brush against her skin. She looked down at him, and felt a sudden rush of feeling that had absolutely nothing to do with the vivid bursts of pleasure that his fingers and mouth were provoking.

Careful! she warned herself shakily. This could get very complicated, unless you back off right now.

It took much more effort than she had expected to make herself draw back from him. Nathan didn't look particularly pleased at her obvious reluctance to let this go any further but, to her relief, he seemed to accept it. And he didn't make any more attempts to touch her.

Rather hurriedly, knowing that she ought to get away from him while she had the chance, Rose scrambled to her feet. 'I think I'll go back to the house now.'

'I'll come with you,' Nathan said, to her consternation.

'I'll be quite all right on my own,' she gabbled. 'Why don't you—er—stay here for a while?'

He gave her an odd smile. 'But I don't want to. Anyway, you go too many places on your own. That isn't always wise.'

Rose wasn't at all sure that it was very wise to be here on this deserted beach with this particular man.

She didn't think she had better say that out loud, though. Instead, she lifted her head a little defiantly.

'I came all the way to England on my own, and so far I haven't run into any trouble.' Discounting everything that had happened since she had met Nathan Hayward, of course.

He looked at her curiously. 'Why *did* you come by yourself? Surely you could have found a friend to come with you? Or did it have something to do with that man you were involved with in Washington?'

'Partly,' she admitted. 'He made me feel inadequate, and I didn't like that because I knew that I wasn't. Coming on this trip on my own was a way of proving that to myself. Of proving I could stand on my own two feet and cope with whatever problems I came up against.'

He suddenly smiled at her. It always threw her when he did that. Charm blazed out of him, along with that smile, and it really was a devastating combination.

'And am I turning out to be one of the problems that you're trying to prove you can cope with?'

Rose wasn't at all sure how to answer that. Whatever she said, she was sure it was going to sound wrong. In the end, she said nothing at all. Instead, she began to shake the sand out of her clothes. It really was time she got dressed.

'You can't put those on,' Nathan told her. 'They're too grubby and full of sand. Here, take my shirt.'

He had slid out of it by the time he had finished speaking. Rose hesitated as he held it out to her. Wearing something that still held the warmth of his body—it was just a little too intimate for her liking.

'I don't have to get dressed at all,' she said, with much more bravado than she felt. 'I can walk back to the house just the way I am. If it doesn't bother you, of course,' she finished, in a tone that somehow came out a lot more challenging than she had intended.

'It bothers me in the very pleasantest way possible,' Nathan replied, his eyes bright again now. 'But I can't promise that we won't run into someone who won't be a little more shocked. The North Devon coastal path runs close by here. Plenty of walkers come this way. And then there are the rambling clubs—this cove is a place they often make for.'

Rose took the hint, and grabbed hold of his shirt. Wearing it was just as unsettling as she had suspected it might be. And as they walked back to Lyncombe Manor in the hot, bright sunshine, it occurred to her that this might be a very good time to leave, before Nathan Hayward found a way of disturbing her even more deeply.

CHAPTER SIX

ROSE didn't leave, of course. She loved Lyncombe Manor too much. Every time she set foot inside the house, it wove its spell over her all over again.

And Nathan Hayward? she asked herself uneasily. Was he beginning to weave a spell over her, as well?

Definitely not, she decided firmly. She was a little star-struck, that was all. She had never met anyone quite like him before.

She felt as if she needed to get away from both the house, and Nathan, for just a couple of hours, though. Some time on her own would help her to get things back into perspective again.

She didn't think Nathan could object if she took the afternoon off. During the last few days, she had worked almost non-stop. Anyway, she didn't really care if he did object. She was going out for a while, and that was that.

Even though her car had been standing in the shade, the interior was stiflingly hot. The temperature seemed to be climbing a little higher each day, and she wondered how much longer this hot spell was going to last. She wound down the windows, and started up the engine. Then she drove away from Lyncombe Manor.

Rose had no clear idea where she was going. In the end, she simply headed towards the coast, hoping it might be fractionally cooler there.

She ended up at a small seaside resort and managed to find somewhere to park the car. Then she strolled down towards the beach.

The wide stretch of golden sand was filled with children noisily making the most of the heatwave, rushing around in skimpy swimsuits, brandishing buckets and spades, and dripping ice-cream everywhere. In contrast, most of the adults were flopped out on the hot sand, too lethargic to move.

Rose sunbathed for a while, finding a small patch of beach that was relatively empty, and stretching out in the heat. She felt too restless to lie still for long, though. With a small sigh, she scrambled back to her feet and gathered her things together. Then she headed towards the small high street. She might as well have a look around the shops, while she was here.

Halfway up the high street was a record shop. Rose found herself pausing in front of it; then, acting on an impulse that she couldn't really explain, she pushed open the door and went inside.

The music cassettes were arranged alphabetically. It was all too easy to find the 'K's. Her eyes skimmed along the row, and then stopped halfway along. They had three tapes of songs by Jancis Kendall. Rose reached out, hesitated, and then more firmly picked out one of them.

A moment later, she wished she had resisted the temptation to walk into the shop. There was a depressingly good photo of Jancis Kendall on the front of the cassette. Rose found herself staring at a pair of cool blue eyes set in a perfectly shaped face, framed by a fall of blonde hair that was so pale that it was almost white.

Not the kind of face that anyone would easily forget. And Rose was quite sure that Nathan *hadn't* forgotten it. All the same, she walked over to the counter and bought the tape.

When she got back to her car, she took out the small card that listed the tracks on the tape. There, at the bottom, it said in very clear print, 'All songs by Nathan Hayward'.

Rose stared at that one short phrase for quite some time. Knowing that he had written all of Jancis Kendall's material was one thing. Seeing it set down in black and white like that was somehow quite different. It forced her to see him in a new light. Not just the man who had locked her in the cellar, argued with her, and then, astonishingly, decided that he liked kissing her. This Nathan Hayward was still a stranger; a man who had written songs that had sold all over the world; someone who had been obsessively involved with the person who had sung those songs.

Rose felt more disturbed than she cared to admit. It was as if she had managed to block out that part of Nathan's life, until now. Or at least pushed it to the very back of her mind, where she could fairly successfully ignore it. This tape was all too real, though. In an odd way, it represented the relationship that had existed between Nathan and Jancis Kendall.

With a deep frown, she shoved the tape into the glove compartment, so that it was was out of sight. But as she slowly drove back to Lyncombe Manor, she couldn't seem to stop herself from thinking about it. When she finally drew up in front of the house, she took the tape out of the compartment again, and slid it into the pocket of her jeans.

There was no sign of Nathan as she made her way to the kitchen, and she was rather glad of that. She made herself a salad, and sat and ate it. Then, after she had cleared away the dishes, she made her way slowly to the small sitting-room at the back of the manor. She remembered seeing a portable cassette player standing on top of the bureau in the corner.

Rose walked through the doorway and found the cassette player standing just where she had expected it to be. She gave a small sigh. It looked as if she couldn't find any more excuses for not playing the tape.

She slid it into the player, and switched it on. Then, because she couldn't sit still and listen to it, she wandered restlessly around the room as Jancis Kendall's deep, distinctive voice began to sing the slow, spine-tingling introduction to the first song.

By the time she had finished listening to the first side of the tape, Rose felt very funny inside. Some of the songs were familiar and a couple were new to her, but they all seemed to hit her in exactly the same way. She swallowed hard and told herself that music always seemed to find the vulnerable spots inside of you. All the same, her hand wasn't quite steady as she turned the tape over, and pressed the button to play the other side.

Jancis Kendall's voice filled the room again, and Rose found it all too easy to picture that flawless face and the shimmering pale hair. In fact, she seemed to have just about everything—except, perhaps, a soul.

The second track began, and Rose briefly closed her eyes as Nathan's intricate phrases were flawlessly delivered by that low, perfectly pitched voice. She could feel a tight lump growing in her throat, although she didn't have any idea why it was there. She also knew that, in a moment, she was going to have to switch the tape off. She just couldn't listen to any more of it right now.

As she began to move towards the cassette player, though, the door was suddenly flung open with such force that, afterwards, she was surprised it hadn't broken right off its hinges. Then Nathan roared into the room like an out-of-control cyclone.

His explosive entry made her literally jump into the air with fright. And when she saw the look on his face, her heart began to thump even more wildly and loudly.

'Where the hell did you get that tape from?' he bellowed at her.

Rose's throat had gone so dry that she couldn't get out an answer. Instead, she just gave a hoarse croak, which seemed to make Nathan even more furious.

He seized hold of her shoulders and shook her quite savagely. 'Where did you get it?' he shouted at her again.

With a huge effort, she managed to find her voice. 'I—I b-bought it,' she stuttered.

He drew his hand back, as if her reply made him so angry that he wanted to hit her. At the last moment he lowered it again, and instead glared at her with such fierceness that his slate-grey eyes seemed to be ablaze.

'Why did you do a damned stupid thing like that?' he demanded.

Rose had shrunk back instinctively from that initial onslaught. Now, though, she was beginning to recover herself slightly, and she glowered back at him.

'I can spend my money on whatever I please! I don't have to ask your permission before I buy something.'

'No,' Nathan said grimly. 'But you do have to ask permission before you play that particular tape in this house.'

'And if I *had* asked?' Rose said with growing boldness.

'I'd have said no!'

'Why? Because you don't want to hear your own music? Or is it Jancis Kendall's voice that you can't stand listening to?'

Rose was amazed that she had found the courage to say such a thing. A moment later she wished she had kept her mouth shut. Nathan's mouth twisted with a fresh surge of anger, and his slate-grey eyes became almost black with the force of the emotions that shook him.

'I don't have to explain my reasons to you. And I don't have to listen to any more of this trash!'

With one swift movement, he picked up the cassette player, wrenching the plug out of the socket at the same time. Then he hurled it straight through the nearest window, the sound of shattering glass seeming to echo round and round the room. After the last piece of glass had crashed to the ground and splintered, the silence that filled the room somehow seemed almost as shocking as the violence that had whirled through it only moments before.

Rose stood there and simply shook. All her courage, her defiance, had simply vanished.

Even Nathan seemed rather stunned by his own actions. He stared at the gaping hole in the window, at the jagged shards of glass on the floor. Then he muttered something under his breath. Finally, he swung round and strode very swiftly out of the room.

Once he had gone, Rose let out a very shaky breath. A couple of times, she had thought that she was beginning to know this man. Now she realised that she didn't know him at all.

Extraordinarily, though, she still wasn't frightened of him. Despite the smashed glass and the sudden burst of violence, she hadn't been truly scared. She had nearly jumped out of her skin, of course, and she was still shaking a little with reaction after that great outburst of anger, but that was just a natural reaction to the intensity of emotion that had been generated. Even when he had raised his hand to her, she had never, for one moment, believed that he would actually hit her.

'You're crazy,' she told herself ruefully. 'You've *got* to be crazy. Anyone in their right mind would head straight for the front door and then keep running until they were well away from here!'

There wasn't much point in trying to clear up the glass. Most of it had fallen outside, anyway, bursting outwards as the cassette player had sailed through the window.

There wasn't much point in trying to retrieve the cassette player, either. That was one machine that was never going to play tapes again!

Slowly, her legs still feeling wobbly, Rose left the room. The house seemed silent and empty, and oddly peaceful. It was almost as if that brief, violent scene had never happened.

She went out to sit in the courtyard, suddenly feeling in need of some fresh air. The sun was beginning to set now, but it was still hot and humid outside. A faint headache was beginning to gather behind her temples, and when she rubbed her forehead with her fingertips, she could feel the tension there.

'Well, that's hardly surprising!' she murmured to herself wryly. 'It's been quite a day.'

She let her hands fall back into her lap, and breathed in the scented air. Roses, a late-blooming honeysuckle, old-fashioned pinks and a cluster of stocks were all releasing their fragrance as dusk began to gather. She felt her taut muscles begin to relax a little. Then they instinctively stiffened again as Nathan slid on to the seat beside her.

'I think that I owe you an apology,' he said in a dry voice.

'Not really,' replied Rose, in an even tone. 'As you've told me more than once, this *is* your house. If you want to throw a cassette player through the window, then you're perfectly entitled to do just that.'

She knew that he was looking at her. She wouldn't meet his gaze, but instead kept staring steadily ahead.

'You're an extraordinary girl,' Nathan said at last. 'Anyone else would have packed their bags and run by now.'

'I did consider it. But I didn't see why I should leave just because you're having a few problems with your temper.'

'Believe it or not, I've generally been fairly relaxed and laid back since I came to Lyncombe Manor. I've only had a handful of bad patches—but, unfortunately, you seem to have been around for every one of them. Or perhaps you're somehow causing them,' he added thoughtfully.

'That's a ridiculous thing to say!' Rose retorted indignantly.

'Is it?' He shrugged. 'I don't know. Things seem to have changed rather dramatically since you arrived. Maybe it's just a coincidence—but, somehow, I don't think so.'

This time, she did look at him. 'What do you want me to do?' she asked in a small voice. 'Go away?'

'I didn't say that,' he replied equably. 'I didn't even say that I disliked the changes that seem to be happening. I might be losing my temper rather a lot lately, but at least it makes me feel alive.'

Rose found it hard to believe that she was having this fairly amicable conversation with him, especially so soon after that fraught scene such a short time ago. 'Why couldn't you be this reasonable when you heard me playing that tape?' she said, with a small frown. 'All you had to do was ask me to turn it off. There was no need to throw the whole thing through the window!'

'When I heard Jancis's voice, something inside me just snapped,' he said slowly. 'This house has never been touched by her. I wanted to keep it that way.'

'You can't go on avoiding her for the rest of your life.'

'I don't intend to. I want this house to stay free of her, though. I need a place that hasn't been tarnished by her touch.'

But Rose wasn't convinced. If he was really over his obsessive relationship with Jancis, why had he had that over-the-top reaction at just the sound of her voice?

Suddenly, she was very sick of the subject of Jancis Kendall. She would be more than pleased if she never heard that name again. 'I've got a headache,' she said, rubbing her forehead tiredly. 'I'm going to take a couple of aspirin, and go to bed.' She thought that he might try to keep her with him for a little longer, but he didn't even look at her as she stood up. 'Goodnight,' she muttered.

'Goodnight—Rose,' he replied absently, as if, for a moment, he hadn't been thinking of her at all.

Rose escaped to her room, gulped down the aspirin and then flopped on to the bed. She meant to close her aching eyes for just a couple of minutes before hauling herself off to the bathroom for a long, relaxing soak. Instead, she fell into a deep sleep and didn't wake up again until morning.

She felt hot and sticky after sleeping in her clothes all night. The temperature was already soaring, although it was still fairly early in the morning, and the sun was shining with its usual dazzling brightness.

Rose wriggled out of her clothes and, after a very cool bath, felt slightly more refreshed. She put on a pair of shorts and the thinnest T-shirt she could find. Then she went down to have a quick breakfast before starting work on the garden again.

Because of the heat, she spent the morning clearing one of the shady areas around the pond. Even outside, it felt airless and oppressively humid. Rose liked the sun, but she was beginning to feel that you could have too much of a good thing. She was almost longing for the sight of a cloud in that relentlessly blue sky.

She decided Nathan must be either out, or in another part of the house, because there was no sign of him when she went in for lunch. That suited her very well. After last night's dramatic little scene, she was quite happy to spend some time on her own. Perhaps she had led a rather sheltered life, but she wasn't used to people throwing things straight through the nearest window!

After lunch, it was just too hot to work, even in the shade. Rose retreated to one of the small sitting-rooms, where she settled at the table by the window and began to write a letter to her parents.

She had already written to them since her arrival at Lyncombe Manor, letting them know where she was and what she was doing. Now she found herself telling them a great deal about Nathan. The words poured down on to the paper, and she finally ended with a long paragraph in which she listed all the reasons why she should stay on at Lyncombe Manor for a while longer, yet without once mentioning the real reason why she didn't want to go. It came down to one very simple sentence. She didn't want to leave Nathan Hayward.

When Rose finally read it through, she gave a small sigh and then tore the whole thing up. She couldn't possibly send them a letter like that. It would worry them half to death. It worried *her* when she realised just how much she had admitted in that sudden outpouring.

She set about writing a second letter which was light and chatty and amusing. Nathan was only mentioned very briefly, and anyone reading it might think that she saw virtually nothing of him.

Rose nearly tore that letter up, too. In the end, though, she shoved it into an envelope and addressed it. Her parents would probably rather read all that light froth than hear nothing from her at all.

A glance out of the window warned her that the heat-wave might be at last coming to an end. Great heavy clouds were piling up on the horizon, and the air had that peculiar stillness that often preceded a spectacular storm.

It was still too hot to work. Her hair was clinging damply to her forehead, and she thought she might take another nearly cold bath. It was about the only thing that would cool her down.

At that moment the door opened and Nathan came into the room. 'I've been looking for you,' he said without preamble. 'Can you sing?'

'Sing?' repeated Rose, her eyebrows shooting up in surprise. 'Well—not really.'

'Of course you can. Everyone can sing. Come with me,' he ordered.

He strode out of the room without waiting to see if she was following him. Rose shot an exasperated look at his rapidly departing back. Then, with a resigned sigh, she trotted along behind him.

Nathan led her to the room which contained the piano. Seating himself behind it, he ran his fingers lightly over the keys. Then he looked up at her. 'Can you read music?'

'No,' she said promptly.

He gave a small, irritable growl. Then he thrust a sheet of paper at her. 'Then just read the words on this. I'll play the first few lines of the song over a couple of times, until you get the hang of how it goes.'

As he played, Rose tried to fit the words scrawled on the sheet of paper to the music. In fact, it was much easier than she had thought it would be. And the song, although simple, had the unmistakable Nathan Hayward touch, with small subtleties built into the tune, lifting it right out of the ordinary.

'Do you think you've got it now?' asked Nathan, after playing it through for the third time.

'I think so,' she said, although not very confidently. Then she fidgeted rather restlessly. 'Look, why don't you sing it through yourself? I don't think I'm going to be much good at this.'

'It's written for a female voice,' he replied impatiently. 'And you're the only female around.' He picked out the opening notes. 'Right, let's try it.'

Rose managed the first line, and knew perfectly well that it sounded awful.

'You're singing too high,' Nathan told her, with a growing frown. 'Pitch your voice lower.'

'It doesn't go lower,' she retorted.

He gave a distinct sigh of exasperation. 'Then I'll change the key.'

They tried it again, and Rose got right through the first part of the song this time. It didn't sound any better, though.

'I told you that I couldn't sing,' she said defensively.

'You're just not trying. And I think you could sing lower, if you made an effort. Let's try it again in the original key.'

But Rose muffed most of the bottom notes and, halfway through, Nathan slammed his fingers down on the keys in a discordant jangle of sound. 'Not like that! Like *this*.'

He sang it through himself, and, despite the sticky heat that filled the room, Rose's skin grew cold, because she finally realised who he was trying to make her sound like.

'Why are you doing this?' she accused a little wildly, as he finished singing the first section. She threw the sheet of paper with the words on it on to the floor. 'After all, you're the one who said you didn't want any trace of her in this house!'

Nathan stared at her blankly. 'What on earth are you talking about?'

Rose shook her head in disbelief. 'You don't even *know* you're doing it, do you?'

'Doing what?' he demanded.

'Trying to turn me into another Jancis Kendall! Well, it won't work, you can't do it. I don't look like her, I don't sing like her, and I sure as hell don't want to be her! Keep writing songs for her, if that's what turns you on, but don't ever again ask me to sing them. She's your obsession, not mine!'

Nathan's expression changed from disbelief to sheer blazing anger. Before he had a chance to say anything, though, Rose tore out of the room, slamming the door hard behind her. Then, in case he took it into his head to come after her, she just kept going, racing out of the house and into the garden.

The sun had completely disappeared now, blotted out by towering clouds that were ominously black. Rose ignored the weather. She just wanted to run and run, leaving behind the increasingly tormenting image of a woman she had never met, but who seemed to be intruding more and more on her life.

The first giant spots of rain hit her as she sprinted round the pond, towards the lower end of the garden. The spreading branches of a massive copper beech offered protection, but she ignored them. The rain stopped for a few seconds, as if it couldn't quite decide whether to fall or not. Then it began to come down much harder. At the same time, a vivid streak of lightning illuminated the darkening sky.

The following clap of thunder was a long, low rumble that warned of more violent explosions to come. But Rose wasn't scared of storms. She was running away from something quite different.

More black clouds swept in, and the rain rapidly turned into an absolute torrent. In just seconds, Rose was drenched to the skin. She never considered, for even an instant, going back to the house, though. Instead, she headed rather blindly in the direction of the path that led along the valley to the cove.

Before she had taken more than a few steps, a hand descended heavily on her shoulder, bringing her to an abrupt halt. Then it jerked on her arm, swinging her round.

Rose found herself facing Nathan, who was as breathless and dripping wet as she was. 'Where the hell do you think you're going?' he demanded tersely.

'That's none of your damned business!' she shouted back at him. 'I can go where I please. And right now, I don't want to be anywhere near that house—or near you!'

His brows drew together in a black frown. 'Because of that song?'

'Because of that song. And because of the way you wanted me to sing it!'

Nathan gave her an impatient shake. 'That song wasn't written for Jancis. And I wasn't trying to make you sing like her.'

Rose glared at him furiously, glad of the torrential rain because it disguised the wet brightness of her eyes. 'Well, you could certainly have fooled me!' she threw back at him. 'I could hear her voice, all the time I was trying to sing it. It was *exactly* the type of song that you used to write for her.'

Nathan pushed his saturated hair out of his eyes, in an irritable gesture. 'I can't suddenly start writing

in a different style, just because Jancis isn't around
any more. When I sit down at the piano, I hear the
song inside my head, and I have to set it down exactly
the way I hear it. The music forms in my mind in a
certain way and that's what makes it *mine*.' When
Rose didn't say anything, he gave her another shake,
a little more roughly this time. 'I can't change the way
I write,' he repeated. 'Don't you understand that? But
I don't think of Jancis when I write—not any more.
And these new songs certainly weren't written for her.'

Rose was only half listening. Whenever she heard
Jancis's name, shutters seemed to close down inside
her head, as if in an effort to shut out what was being
said.

'I don't really care who you wrote the songs for,'
she muttered at last. 'And let go of me! I want to get
away from here.'

She tried to wrench her arm free, but Nathan's grip
merely tightened. 'You can't stay out here,' he growled
at her. 'You're soaked.'

'It doesn't matter. Just leave me alone. I'm *all right*.'

His slate-grey eyes fixed on her. 'If you were all
right, you wouldn't be out here in the pouring rain.
I'm taking you back to the house.'

'I don't want to go!' she insisted vehemently, but
he simply ignored her protests. Keeping a vice-like grip
on her arm, he began to drag her back towards
Lyncombe Manor.

The storm was sweeping nearer now, with spectacular bolts of lightning zipping across the sky, followed
by ear-splitting crashes of thunder. Although it was
still daylight, it seemed more like dusk, as the black
clouds rolled overhead. Now and then, Rose caught
a vivid glimpse of Nathan's face as it was illuminated

by the brilliant lightning, and it sent nervous shivers right up her spine. He looked unexpectedly grim, and his mouth was very taut. For once, he seemed almost like a stranger.

He *is* a stranger, Rose told herself a little frantically. She knew she was lying, though. There had been something very familiar about him, from the very first. Something that had made her stay when she knew she ought to have run away; something that kept her from ever being truly scared of him, even now, when he was in a mood that she had never seen before.

The house loomed up in front of them, little more than a black shape seen through the heavy curtain of rain. Nathan dragged her in through the kitchen, and Rose found that it was dark inside. The storm was almost overhead now, blotting out all the light, and shaking the very walls with its force.

Nathan didn't stay in the kitchen. Instead, he kept on moving, pulling her through the passageway that led right through the house to the entrance hall, and then hauling her up the stairs.

'Where are we going?' gasped Rose, managing to drag in just enough breath to speak coherently.

'Somewhere I can prove to you, once and for all, that I'm not confusing you with Jancis Kendall,' he replied grimly.

They were at the top of the stairs now. A few yards further on, he opened a door and pushed her into the room beyond. Then he closed the door again very firmly behind them.

Rose glanced round and knew at once where she was. The master bedroom—and she had been brought here by the master of this house.

'No,' she said at once.

'Yes,' Nathan contradicted her in a voice that was very soft and yet absolutely clear.

'I don't want to,' she insisted. Yet there was an unnerving lack of conviction in her tone.

Nathan simply ignored her. Instead, he began to pull off her soaked T-shirt. She knew that she ought to be resisting him, but found herself holding her arms up so that he could get it off more easily. Nathan grunted in approval; then he swiftly set about removing the rest of her clothes.

The room was in semi-darkness because of the storm, only lit intermittently by the dazzling flashes of lightning. Rose's head throbbed slightly as the thunder cracked and rumbled all around them, and she felt as if none of this were at all real. In fact, she was quite certain it couldn't actually be happening.

Then Nathan's hands found her small breasts, and that certainly felt real enough. His skin was as wet as hers, but it wasn't cold. She could feel the warmth pulsing through his palms as they cupped her, and then rubbed lightly against her.

He was impatient to move on, though; she could feel the restlessness rising in him, the increased heat of his body. He unfastened her cotton shorts, and then knelt before her as he pushed them downwards. His mouth drifted over the flat plane of her stomach, setting her muscles quivering in its wake, and then slid over the silky skin of her thighs as he bent still lower.

Rose began to tremble. No one had ever touched her like this before. She had endured some clumsy fumbling, which she had never really enjoyed, and hadn't realised that a man's mouth and fingers could be this light and gentle.

Nathan stood up again and began to shrug off his own clothes. At the same time, he bent his head and kissed her, so that the contact between them was constant.

Another vivid flash of lightning revealed the lean lines of his body to her, and she found herself wishing it were clear daylight, so that she could see him better. Yet it was curiously tantalising, just catching brief glimpses of him as the lightning momentarily illuminated the room.

He was breathing hard now, but so was she. That was new, as well. She wasn't used to this rapid arousal of her senses. Rose began to wonder how many more unfamiliar sensations she was going to experience before this was all over, but her whirling thoughts were interrupted by the sudden closeness of Nathan's body, moving in on her.

Wet skin moved easily against wet skin, increasing the tactile pleasure they found in each other. They were on the bed now, although Rose didn't remember how they had got here. It was another massive four-poster, the heavy canopy looming above them.

Very romantic, she thought hazily. Everyone should make love in a four-poster bed. Then the increased pressure of Nathan's hot body drove all other thoughts from her head.

'It's been too long,' he said in a tight, husky voice. 'Can't wait. Sorry.'

But, to her amazement, Rose found herself already caught up in the spiralling storm of intense delight. And although it was all over in just a few dazzling minutes, they were the longest, most exquisitely pleasurable minutes she had ever experienced in her entire life.

CHAPTER SEVEN

THEY both lay very still for some time. The storm outside the window continued to rage, though, and Rose soon realised that the storm inside the room wasn't yet over.

Nathan stirred and let his hand rest against the curve of her hip. 'I didn't think it would be quite like this,' he said in a throaty voice.

'Quite like what?' whispered Rose.

'Different.'

She wasn't sure she liked that. 'Different in what sort of way?' she asked uncertainly.

Unexpectedly, Nathan smiled. 'In every way possible.' His hand moved upwards, lingering over the inward curve of her waist.

Rose found herself trying to see his face more clearly. She could only tell so much from the tone of his voice. The dark clouds were still circling overhead, blotting out most of the natural light.

She began to feel oddly unsure of herself, despite what had happened between them. 'I wish we could put the light on,' she blurted out.

Nathan reached out and switched on the lamp beside the bed. Nothing happened. 'Power cut,' he said. 'No lights, I'm afraid.' He looked at her curiously. 'Why do you suddenly want the light on?'

'You'd be able to see me,' she said in a low voice. 'Here, in the darkness, I could be anyone. You wouldn't even have to close your eyes to pretend I was someone else.'

She hadn't meant to say anything of the sort, and immediately wished that her tongue hadn't run away with her. He would get angry now, and everything would be ruined.

Nathan propped himself up on one elbow, so that he was looking down at her. His features remained relaxed, though, and his voice, when he eventually spoke, was quite calm. 'I know exactly who you are. You're Rose, with the small, beautiful breasts, and the long, long legs. I haven't, even for one second, forgotten who I'm with. And I don't want to pretend that you're someone else. I'll never want to do that.'

His fingers lightly began to caress her again, causing small shivers of pleasure to ripple immediately over her skin.

'You like everything that I do to you, don't you?' he said in a pleased tone.

'Yes,' she admitted simply. She was aching to touch him in return, but he lightly caught hold of her wrists when she reached out to him.

'Not yet,' he instructed huskily. 'I want to be in control a little longer—and I won't be, if you touch me.'

Rose was a little awed by the desire she could arouse in him. And her own body felt beautiful for once. Not long and lanky, and too thin, but sleek and supple, capable of being completely female.

How could one man make her feel so different? she wondered rather dizzily. Why him, and no one else?

Nathan didn't give her a chance to answer her own questions. His fingers tormented and teased until she was gasping under his touch, and then he licked her into total submission. He was allowing her to touch him by this time. At least, he made no attempt to stop her when her hands moved over his lean, hard body, caressing him almost with reverence.

His mouth found hers again, only more roughly than before. These kisses were fiercely demanding, and she understood that his self-control had snapped much more quickly and easily than he had expected, or wanted. It didn't seem to matter, though. She had the feeling that it was *never* going to matter.

The shared pleasure was as intense as before, and only slowly subsided into warm, relaxed exhaustion. As if in harmony with their mood, the storm outside finally began to move away, rolling slowly off into the distance, so that peace gradually returned to Lyncombe Manor. By then, though, neither of them knew anything about it. They were both deeply asleep, curled up together, limbs twined in a tangle, in the huge four-poster bed.

Rose was the first to wake up. She was amazed to find that it was morning. She had slept for hours. *They* had slept for hours, she corrected herself, as she turned her head to look at Nathan, who was still sprawled out beside her.

In the clear, bright light of morning, she found it hard to believe that any of it had really happened. She wasn't a girl who blithely jumped into bed with anyone. In fact, there was only one other bed she had jumped into in her entire life, and she hadn't actually jumped at all. She had gone with deep reluctance, only finally agreeing to it because she had thought it was the only way to keep the relationship going. All that had happened, though, was that she had been made to feel inadequate, and the relationship had failed anyway.

Nathan certainly didn't make her feel inadequate. Quite the opposite, in fact. He had let her see, very clearly, that she could arouse him with great ease. And give him intense satisfaction when that desire reached its peak.

So, what did it all mean? she wondered uneasily.

In fact, Rose had the feeling that she knew very well what it meant, but she didn't want to admit it to herself yet. For a while longer, she would go on pretending that she was puzzled by the whole thing. It might not be very honest, but it would probably be a lot better for her peace of mind.

Nathan stirred at that point, and Rose promptly forgot everything except her anxiety as she waited for his first reaction.

His slate-grey eyes blinked rather sleepily. Then they became much more alert as they fixed on her.

'That was a spectacular storm, wasn't it?' she gabbled with a sudden burst of nervousness, saying the first thing that came into her head.

'I think that the whole night was fairly spectacular,' he replied lazily.

Rose swallowed hard. 'I don't want you to think— I don't usually—well, I mean I don't——'

'Do this kind of thing on a regular basis?' he finished for her with some amusement, as her voice stuttered to a standstill. 'I know that.'

'How?' she asked curiously, forgetting her awkwardness for a few moments.

'I may be rather out of practice, but there was a time when I was very experienced at this sort of thing,' Nathan replied drily.

'And you could tell that I *wasn't* very experienced?' she mumbled.

'Yes,' he agreed. 'But there's no need to look so downcast. It doesn't matter. It isn't in the least important. In fact, I liked it.' His gaze darkened noticeably. 'I liked it very much.'

Rose noticed the change in his face—and in his voice—and rather hurriedly wriggled over to the far side of the bed. She wasn't ready to go through all that again, not yet. Her emotions were still in total turmoil, and she needed time to sort them out before she let this go any further.

She grabbed the sheet and managed to wrap it round her. Then she slid off the bed and edged towards the door. 'I think I'll—er—take a bath,' she said edgily.

'Good idea.' He threw back the covers. 'I'll join you.'

'No!' she yelped. Then she found herself hurriedly looking away from his naked body, which was perfectly ridiculous considering how very close she had been to it all night.

Nathan seemed to be watching her confusion with some amusement. 'Perhaps I'll have a bath later,' he said, his eyes dancing.

Rose let out a silent sigh of relief. All she had to do now was to get out of this room. She fumbled for the door handle, and managed to turn it. 'Well, I'll—er—I'll go and——'

'Take a bath?' he reminded her helpfully.

Rose scowled at him. He was making fun of her now. She held the sheet a little tighter around her, muttered something rather incoherently under her breath, and then backed very rapidly out of the door.

The last glimpse she had of Nathan was of him lying back on the bed, looking very relaxed and grinning from ear to ear. For some reason, it annoyed her that he looked so very pleased with himself.

'Men can be so *smug*,' she told herself crossly. Then she hitched up the sheet and headed quickly towards the bathroom, locking herself in, just in case Nathan took it into his head to ignore her sudden prudishness and try to join her.

The air was much fresher this morning, after the violent storm, but it didn't make Rose's head feel any clearer. Even a nearly cold bath didn't improve matters. Every time her thoughts wandered anywhere near the subject of Nathan, she was engulfed in instant confusion.

You should have kept running last night, she told herself more than once. You shouldn't have let him come anywhere near you.

Yet, ever since she had first set eyes on Nathan Hayward, part of her seemed to have known that she would eventually end up like this. Perhaps it was why she had never made any serious effort to leave the manor. Why she hadn't fought very hard after he had caught hold of her last night.

A deep sigh escaped her. This meant trouble, no matter which way she looked at it. Nathan might want her now, but there had been no talk of a serious relationship. She didn't even know how he felt about her—assuming he felt anything at all, except for a brief surge of desire.

She was beginning to realise how she felt about *him*, though. In fact, she had probably known it for quite some time, but hadn't had the nerve to face up to it.

'Well, you'd better face it now,' she told herself with a nervous grimace. 'And figure out what you're going to do about it!'

She dried herself, and quickly dressed. Then she went down to the kitchen, but found she didn't want any breakfast. In fact, she felt as if it would be a very long while before she could face food of any kind. Instead, she went out into the courtyard and sat in the warm sunshine, beginning to feel distinctly dazed as the full implications of what had happened began to sink in.

About half an hour later, Nathan sauntered out and joined her. As he sat down on the wooden seat, Rose nervously edged away a few inches. He must have noticed it but, to her relief, didn't comment on it. 'How are you planning on spending today?' he asked her in a conversational tone.

'I'm going to clear the flower-bed by the duck pond,' she told him.

'I see.' His voice was thoughtful now. 'In other words, you're going to pretend that it's just a perfectly normal day.'

'It *is* a normal day,' she shot back quickly.

One of his dark eyebrows rose questioningly but he didn't push the point any further. 'If you're going to work in the garden, I might as well spend some time at the piano,' he said at last.

'That sounds like a good idea.'

He turned his head and looked straight at her. 'And how long are you going to keep this up?'

Rose gulped nervously. 'Keep—keep what up?'

'Pretending that last night didn't happen.'

For some reason, his words got to her. 'I know perfectly well that it happened!' she retorted.

'Then why are you behaving like this?'

But Rose didn't want to tell him the truth. It would give him too much of an advantage over her. 'I suppose I just wasn't ready for it,' she mumbled. 'It was too soon. I wasn't expecting it.'

There was no amusement in his slate-grey eyes now. 'I think that you've been expecting it ever since the day you moved in here,' he told her softly.

His perceptiveness highly alarmed her. If he knew that, what else did he know?

'How can you say that?' she said with sudden fierceness. 'Soon after I came here, you told me that you weren't interested in me, that I wasn't your type. Then I had to hear all about your obsession with Jancis Kendall, and how *she* was the one you always wanted in your bed. How was I to know you'd take me for a substitute, since she wasn't around any longer?'

Rose had never meant to say any such thing, but the words had just seemed to pour out of her. And it wasn't until she had actually said them out loud that she realised that this was what she had been afraid of all along. That Nathan wouldn't look at her twice if Jancis Kendall were still around.

He growled something angrily under his breath.

'I didn't hear that,' she said tensely.

'I was just wondering how a girl as bright as you can also be so incredibly stupid!'

Rose got angrily to her feet. 'Well, I suppose it just takes a lot of practice!'

She was about to stalk off, but Nathan also got up and laid a restraining hand on her arm. Rose tried to shake it off, but his fingers gripped her too firmly.

'I don't want you to go like this,' he said tightly.

'Why not?' she challenged him. 'Do you really care, one way or the other?'

His face altered, taking on a darker hue. 'Rose, don't spoil things,' he warned.

'As far as I'm concerned, there's nothing to spoil,' she threw back at him defiantly. 'We had one good night together, and that's it! I don't think that either of us should try and make it into something that it isn't.'

His grip had slackened now, as if she was finally beginning to get through to him. 'You really feel like that about it?' he said tautly.

'Of course,' she lied. Better he should think that than realise just how much he was beginning to get to her.

'Then you'd better go and carry on with your gardening,' he said, his tone suddenly distant. 'You're obviously more interested in that than you are in me.'

Rose didn't move for a moment. What was she doing? she thought with a spurt of panic. If there was a chance in a million that this would turn into something good, wasn't it better to take it, and to hell with her pride and her stupid fears?

But when she turned back to Nathan, she knew that her chance had gone. His face was now as distant as his voice. No more lazy amusement, gentle teasing, words whispered softly and intimately in the darkness. She had just ruined whatever they might have had going for them. And why? Because her obsession with Jancis Kendall was threatening to become as uncontrollable as Nathan's had once been. She slowly walked away, and he made no effort to call her back.

The rest of the day passed slowly and drearily. Rose could hardly believe that, just a few hours ago, she had lived through that long and magical night. She stayed in the garden for most of the time, but she couldn't concentrate on anything she was doing. She pulled up flowers instead of weeds, hacked down bushes instead of gently pruning them, and occasionally found tears dropping on to the ground that had already been soaked by last night's rain.

'This is ridiculous,' she told herself more than once, sniffing hard. 'How can you get this upset over someone you've known for such a short time?'

The answer, of course, was painfully obvious. But, because she still didn't want to face it, she pushed it to the very back of her mind and made a determined effort to ignore it.

She stayed out in the garden until late in the evening, when the light finally began to fade. She had been back into the house only once, to grab a quick sandwich and a drink. Although she still hadn't been in the least hungry, she had hoped the food might help to dispel the awful empty feeling inside of her. It didn't, though. It simply seemed to stick in her throat, threatening to choke her.

As the last of the light faded, Rose reluctantly trailed into the house. For the first time since her arrival, Lyncombe Manor failed to cast its usual spell over her. After a quick shower and a change of clothes, she forced down some more food. Then she decided to escape back to her own rooms, before Nathan put in an appearance.

She hadn't seen him all day. When she had occasionally moved nearer to the house, though, she had heard the sound of music drifting out of the open windows of the room which held the piano. Obviously, he was working on his new collection of songs, and had managed to put her right out of his mind.

Rose trudged wearily up the stairs that led to the east wing. It was almost dark now, but she didn't bother to switch on any lights. This house was becoming so familiar to her that she felt she could have found her way around it blindfolded.

Because of the gathering shadows, she didn't see Nathan waiting for her at the top of the stairs. When he finally stepped out in front of her, she jumped violently. Then, ignoring her thumping heart, she said in a stiff voice, 'What are you doing here?'

She couldn't see Nathan's face very clearly, so it was impossible to tell what he was thinking. When he spoke, though, his voice certainly sounded very relaxed. He seemed to have found a way of getting rid of all that tension that had built up between them in the garden this morning.

'I thought I'd come and ask you where you intend to sleep tonight,' he said, his eyes briefly glittering even in the darkness.

Rose gave a small inner shiver. She supposed she should have expected this, but she hadn't. And that meant she wasn't ready for it. 'I'd prefer to sleep in my own bed,' she said in a fixed tone.

'All the beds in this house can sleep two people quite comfortably,' Nathan remarked.

She suddenly became very angry. 'You seem to be assuming rather a lot!'

'Such as?'

'Such as the fact that you would even be welcome!' she retorted.

Nathan's voice lowered to a soft purr. 'Oh, I think that I'd be welcome.' Then his tone changed again.

'Things were fine between us last night, Rose. If something's gone wrong since then, then let's try and put it right.'

For just a moment, Rose was unbearably tempted. Then the spectre of Jancis Kendall began to rise up in her mind again. She was the ghost of the past; and, no matter how much Nathan denied that he wanted Jancis back, Rose couldn't seem to convince herself that she *was* a ghost. What if there were three people in that bed tonight? Herself, Nathan, and a husky-voiced singer he couldn't forget?

Another shiver shook Rose. Part of her knew that she was being irrational, but she just couldn't seem to stop. Something had happened to her last night, and she wasn't quite the same person today. And this new person wasn't willing to share Nathan—would rather give him up altogether than have only a part of him, while the rest belonged to a blonde-haired woman with no soul.

Nathan was watching her intently, although she knew he couldn't see her face any more clearly than she could see his.

'I wish I knew what was going through your head right now,' he said slowly, at last.

'I was just thinking that I was very tired, and would like to get some sleep,' she said rather jerkily, the lies seeming to stick to her tongue.

He shook his head. 'No, that wasn't what you were thinking,' he said with total conviction. 'I know you, Rose. I know when you're lying.'

'You do *not* know me,' she said with a sudden flash of anger. 'I'm not even sure that you *want* to know me.'

Incredulity spread across his face. 'How can you say that, after last night?'

'We slept together, that's all. That's got nothing to do with knowing someone!'

Nathan shook his head slowly. 'If you really believe that, then you've got a great deal more still to learn. OK, sex can be impersonal. I know that better than anyone! But what happened between us last night was *not* impersonal. It was very good and very intimate, and we discovered things about each other that we probably couldn't have found out any other way. I certainly don't regret what happened.'

'Well, I do!'

The words came out before she could stop them, and she would have traded ten years of her life for the chance to take them back again. Too late now, though. And too late to deny that she had meant it. Nathan's eyes were already alight with a great flood of anger.

'Then here's something else for you to regret!' he said in a tight voice.

He made no attempt to be gentle this time. His mouth inflicted bruising kisses, and his hands moved over her as if he no longer cared who she was: Rose Caldwell, whom he had shared his home—and his bed—with; who had begun to get closer to him than any other person since the break-up of his relationship with Jancis Kendall.

Rose quickly discovered that she hated it when he touched her like this. It aroused her body—with his experience, he could hardly fail to do that!—but not her heart. His fingers roughly caressed the aching tips of her breasts, and she felt a pleasure that wasn't really a pleasure at all. Just a vivid sensation that registered on her nerve-ends, but nowhere else.

His mouth moved lower, as if he was determined to subject every inch of her to this savagely sensual attack. He pulled away her clothes with sudden impatience, and his tongue lashed her hot skin, provoking deep shudders from within her. Yet, at the same time, she shrank back from him. She felt as if she didn't know the man who was doing these things to her.

Nathan wouldn't let go of her, though. His hands moved lower, down to the silky smoothness of her thighs. Rose caught her breath as his hard caresses became more purposeful, the intimacy of his touch all the more shocking because there was no trace of tenderness in it.

Her body began to ache, but it was a perverse kind of desire. She didn't like it; she wanted to draw back from it, but Nathan just pressed harder, his fingers expertly stroking. At the same time, his mouth returned to hers for a kiss that quite literally took her breath away.

When he finally released her mouth, he seemed as breathless as she was. His hands were still on her, though, as relentless as ever. Briefly, he raised his head. 'A part of you is hating this, isn't it?' he challenged her thickly.

'Yes,' she somehow managed to get out.

'You want me, but it's an empty sort of wanting. All sensation, but no feeling.'

If he knew that, why was he doing this to her? she wondered with a surge of bitterness.

He moved still closer, fitting his body against hers so that she became starkly aware that he was hard and aching.

'I could take you to bed right now, and we'd both find some sort of pleasure,' Nathan told her, his voice tight. 'It wouldn't last, and it wouldn't be particularly special, but it's what a lot of people settle for. Is that what you want?'

'Of course I don't!' Her voice was unsteady, but quite adamant.

'Nor do I,' he said grimly, to her surprise. 'Because *this* is impersonal sex, Rose. And this is what it would have been like, if I had simply wanted you last night.' Without any warning, he released her. Relief and disappointment shot through her in equal measures. 'I wanted you to know the difference,' he went on, in a more even tone. 'I thought perhaps you were too inexperienced to realise just how special last night was.'

'I knew it was special,' she said in a rather choked voice. 'But I wasn't certain if *you* knew.'

Nathan looked at her with some amazement. 'Of course I knew. For a start, you're the first woman I've slept with—wanted to sleep with—for over a year. I was beginning to think I was going to remain celibate for the rest of my life! All the desire just seemed to have been knocked out of me. The fact that you could get me going—and push me right over the edge so quickly—makes you someone pretty unique.'

But, somehow, being unique wasn't quite enough. Rose was beginning to realise what it was she really wanted. She wanted to be loved—and, although Nathan obviously had fairly strong feelings towards her, that might be asking just a little too much.

'So, where do we go from here?' she asked in a low voice, suddenly feeling very tired and drained.

'You're going to bed, and I'm going back to my own room,' Nathan said decisively. 'And no,' he added, 'it isn't what I want. You know perfectly well what I want! But there are decisions that are going to have to be made, and sleeping together tonight is only going to confuse things still further. I want you to think about what I've said to you, Rose. We'll talk again, when you're ready, and then perhaps we can finally begin to get things right.'

He turned away from her, and she took an involuntary step forward. 'You're really going back to your own room?' She hadn't meant to say any such thing, and she swallowed hard as he slowly swung back to face her.

'You can make me stay, if you want to,' he told her in a voice that was very husky. 'You won't find it in the least difficult.'

But Rose was already realising that he was right. They needed some time apart, to think things over. 'No,' she mumbled. 'No, you'd better go.'

For a moment, he didn't move. She thought he was going to ignore everything that he had said to her, and simply sweep her off to the bedroom. Then, with an obvious effort, he began to back away again. 'Goodnight, Rose,' he said, in a rather strained tone. 'I'll see you in the morning.'

Even after he had gone, it was some time before she moved. Her muscles seemed to creak with tension as she walked slowly to her room, and she had the feeling that it was going to be a very long night.

When she eventually went to bed, she slept only fitfully, and had odd dreams which left her feeling hot and disturbed. She was relieved when the sun finally slid up into the sky, and she could get up.

She showered and dressed, but as she slowly made her way downstairs she knew that she hadn't managed to reach any firm decisions. There were so many things that she still didn't know, so many things of which she was so horribly uncertain.

She skipped breakfast. Food seemed unimportant at the moment. Instead, she made her way to the great hall, where she found Nathan standing at the window, as if waiting for her.

Despite its size, it was a room she had always felt very comfortable in before. The great fireplace, the warm tones of the panelling, the oak beams overhead, gave it a solid and even homely atmosphere.

This morning, though, she could sense the tension that shimmered in the air. Despite the soft sunshine that filtered through the windows and laid patterned shadows on the stone-flagged floor, her skin felt chilled. Suddenly, she wanted to turn round and run. She wasn't ready yet to talk this over with Nathan. They were all too new, these feelings she had about him. She needed time to get used to them—to get used to her new relationship with *him*—before making decisions of any kind.

But she didn't run. Instead, she walked steadily into the great hall, only pausing when she was a few feet away from Nathan.

He turned to face her, and he looked as if he had had as little sleep as she had. He was smiling, though, and looked unexpectedly relaxed. 'You look as if you're going to your execution!' he teased her lightly. 'I want to talk to you about a couple of things, that's all.'

Rose managed a rather feeble smile back at him, but he seemed to realise at once that it was forced. 'Come and sit down,' he invited, seating himself in one of the high-backed chairs by the window.

She was glad to take the weight off her|slightly shaky legs. She subsided into the chair, and found herself trying not to look directly at him.

'Did you sleep well?' he asked.

'Not very,' she admitted.

Nathan gave a rueful grimace. 'Nor did I. Although that's not very surprising, after what happened between us last night!' He sat back in a relaxed position, and studied her face. After a while, Rose felt a flush of colour rising into her cheeks. Those slate-grey eyes seemed to see far too much!

'If we're going to talk, we need a place to begin,' he said at last. 'Where do you think would be a good starting point, Rose?'

'I don't know,' she mumbled.

'All right, then, I'll suggest a subject which seems fairly relevant, and which we both seem to have been trying to avoid, in one way or another. Jancis Kendall.'

Those last two words seemed to cause an actual twinge of pain along Rose's nerve-ends.

'Anything to say about that particular lady?' he invited softly.

She lifted her head and her violet eyes briefly flared. 'You're the one who introduced the subject! *You* talk about her.'

'I was under the impression that I already had—and at some length. Anyway, I think that I'm over most of my problems concerning Jancis. You're not, though, and I'd like to know why.'

'Because I know about her,' burst out Rose. 'And I know the way you felt about her. If you'd never told me—and I wish you hadn't——' she added with some fervour '—there wouldn't be any problem. But I do know. And now, it always seems to be there, at the back of my mind. I can't forget about her—about the two of you together.'

'It was over a long time ago,' Nathan said levelly.

'Just because it's over, that doesn't mean that it's ended,' Rose said a little shrilly.

His eyes narrowed. 'Are you saying that I lied to you? That I still see her? Still want her?'

'I know you don't see her. But that doesn't mean you don't still—want her.' It cost her an awful effort to get out those last two words.

Nathan was frowning now. 'I thought you were a level-headed girl, Rose. Why can't you leave this alone?'

'I don't know. I don't *want* to keep going over and over it,' she said a little despairingly.

'Then let go of it. Stop dredging up the past. Start to think about the future.'

'I've tried to do that. I can't stop thinking about Jancis Kendall, though. She was such a big part of your life. I feel as if she's always going to be there. And I really don't think I could live with that.'

Nathan got up and prowled across the hall. 'I don't know what the hell to say to you,' he said at last.

'I know I'm behaving stupidly,' Rose said miserably. 'And I know I'm ruining everything. I've never been like this before, and I don't like it, but I can't help it. I feel all the time as if she was the one you really wanted and I'm only second best.'

'Even if I tell you that you're not?'

'It doesn't seem to matter *what* you say. Jancis is still there, spoiling everything. I can't get her out of my head.'

Nathan growled something under his breath. Then he stared out of the window for what seemed like a very long time.

When he swung back to face her, his face had altered and his tone was more decisive. 'I'm going out,' he told her. 'There's a chance I won't be back until quite late. Will you be all right here, on your own?'

Rose wanted to ask him where he was going, but stopped herself at the last moment. 'Yes, I'll be all right,' she said instead, in a subdued voice. She would always be all right at Lyncombe Manor. It wasn't the house that was the problem—it was the man who lived in it.

Nathan strode over to the doorway. Then he came to a halt again and turned back to her. 'You won't run off while I'm away?'

It was more of an order than a question. Rose didn't see how leaving here would solve a single thing, though. She could run a hundred—a thousand—miles, and still not forget Nathan Hayward.

'I'll be here when you get back,' she said quietly. Nathan gave a small nod of satisfaction and then left.

The house seemed very empty after his car had pulled away. For a while, Rose considered breaking her promise and leaving now, while she had the chance. It would be the best time to go. No scenes, no hassle—anyone with any sense would pack their bags, and make a dignified exit.

She even made a half-hearted effort to go up to her room and pack. It was too much effort, though. She didn't seem to have the energy. In the end, she wandered out into the garden, stretched out on a shady patch of grass under one of the trees, and closed her eyes.

She dozed on and off, and in between times she simply gazed up at the clear blue sky. It was still warm, but not the blazingly hot and sticky heat there had been before the storm.

The storm and its aftermath—that was something she didn't really want to think about right now, so she shut her eyes again and tried to go back to sleep. And, after a while, she succeeded.

Late in the afternoon, she had a light meal, which she somehow managed to eat. She wondered what time Nathan would be back. He hadn't said where he was going, or why.

Perhaps he had just wanted to get away from her for a while. He had probably been looking for a short, uncomplicated relationship, and here she was, causing him all these problems. After his stormy relationship with Jancis Kendall, the last thing he needed was a lot more emotional turmoil.

Rose shook her head impatiently. Here she was, back to that old subject again. Why couldn't she stop thinking about Jancis? It was over, over, *over*.

But the ghosts of old lovers never truly go away, whispered a small voice inside her head.

Rose clapped her hands over her ears. She didn't want to hear that! But it was hard to shut out a voice that was coming from her own mind.

Dusk began to close in, and Nathan still hadn't returned. She began to wonder if he was coming back at all. Maybe once he had got away from Lyncombe

Manor, he had realised that his life would be a lot
simpler and easier without her.

Just after full darkness had set in, though, she heard
the sound of a car pulling up outside. Nervously, she
made her way to the entrance hall, reaching it just as
Nathan opened the front door and walked in.

They stood there for some time, simply looking at
each other.

'I wasn't sure you'd still be here,' Nathan said at
last.

'What would you have done if I'd run away?' she
asked in a low voice.

'I'd have come looking for you.'

There was another long silence. Then Nathan came
slowly towards her.

He stopped when he was just a couple of feet away.
His slate-grey eyes fixed on hers, and the expression
in them made her suddenly highly nervous. Without
quite knowing how, Rose knew that he was going to
tell her something that she didn't want to hear.

'I haven't come back alone,' he said, a few moments later.

Her nerve-ends jumped, and her heart began to beat
a little faster. 'Who——' Her voice came out as a dry
croak, and she tried again. 'Who have you brought
with you?'

'I think you already know.'

Rose was horribly afraid that she did, but part of
her refused to believe that he would do anything quite
so crazy.

'I *don't* know,' she said stubbornly.

Nathan kept looking at her with that same steady
gaze. 'I've brought Jancis,' he said levelly. 'It seemed

the only way to sort out the problems that we've run into.'

'I don't want to see her!' Rose shot back at once, with some vehemence.

'I'm not giving you a choice. She's outside in the car, and in just a moment I'm going to bring her in.' Rose began to back away, as if getting ready to dash off, but he swiftly caught hold of her arm. 'You're not going anywhere,' Nathan told her. 'You're staying right here while I fetch Jancis, and then you're going to meet her.'

His eyes briefly blazed down at her, rooting her to the spot. Then he let go of her, and went back out to the car.

Rose couldn't quite believe this was happening, but her shaking legs told her that this wasn't a dream— or a nightmare.

She really was about to come face to face with Jancis Kendall.

CHAPTER EIGHT

NATHAN came back through the door less than a minute later. And this time he was accompanied by someone who seemed strangely familiar, even though Rose had never met her before.

A girl—no, not a girl, a *woman* of stunning physical perfection. Jancis Kendall in the flesh was even more startling than in her photographs.

Rose recognised the fall of pale blonde hair, the flawless skin, and the pale blue eyes. In return, Jancis Kendall was studying Rose with equal curiosity. And something like surprise was registering on that exquisite face.

'I thought you lived here alone,' she said, turning to Nathan.

'I never said that,' replied Nathan, in an expressionless voice.

Rose's eyebrows drew lightly together. He hadn't told Jancis about her? But why not?

Nathan moved over to stand beside her. 'Jancis has apparently been trying to get in touch with me for some time,' he said, his tone still giving absolutely nothing away. 'She wants me to write some material for her. I told her that I've been working on some new songs, and she said she'd like to hear them. Since she had a couple of free days, this seemed like a good time for her to come down and listen to them.'

Rose knew instinctively, though, that it wasn't just songs that Jancis wanted from Nathan. She had come here for a great deal more than that.

'Sorry, I should have introduced you,' went on Nathan. 'Jancis, this is Rose Caldwell. Rose, I think you already know who Jancis is.'

'Yes, I know,' agreed Rose in an even tone.

'And what exactly does Rose do around here?' asked Jancis, her gaze very sharp now as she spoke directly to Nathan, ignoring Rose completely.

'Rose works in the garden,' replied Nathan equably.

'She's an employee?'

'She's a great many things.' And before Jancis had a chance to ask what he meant by that, he went on, 'I'll bring in your luggage, and then show you up to your room. I expect you're tired after the journey.'

'I'm not in the least tired,' said Jancis, her voice returning to its usual silver tone. 'I'd like to see around your beautiful house, Nathan.'

'Well, I'm ready for bed,' Rose cut in quickly, deciding that she had had about as much of this as she could take. 'If you don't mind, I'll say goodnight, and see you in the morning.'

'Where do you sleep, Miss Caldwell?' asked Jancis, speaking straight to her for the first time.

'I have my own rooms in the east wing. Don't worry,' Rose went on flatly, 'I won't disturb you in any way.'

She had no idea what had made her say that. Perhaps it was in response to Jancis's unspoken question. Did she sleep in the same room as Nathan? And even if she didn't, was she likely to turn up at an inopportune moment?

Rose walked steadily towards the stairs. When she gave an involuntary glance back, though, she realised that Jancis had already forgotten about her, dismissed her as unimportant. She was concentrating fully on Nathan now, as he came back into the entrance hall with her luggage. And from the size of the suitcases she had brought with her, Rose guessed that Jancis intended to stay for as long as she possibly could.

Wearily, she made her way up to her own rooms. Where would Jancis sleep tonight? she wondered with a soft sigh. Would she try to move in on Nathan straight away, or would she play it cool and wait for him to make the first approach? Whichever it was, one thing was certain. Jancis Kendall wasn't here because she was interested in some new songs. She was here because she wanted Nathan back again.

Rose had no idea why she was so absolutely sure of that. Perhaps it was her female instincts working overtime, she told herself with a wry grimace. They had certainly begun to bristle as soon as Jancis Kendall had walked in the door of Lyncombe Manor!

Not surprisingly, she didn't sleep well that night. It seemed ages since she had slept more than an hour or so at a stretch. After a quick bath the next morning, she pulled on jeans and a T-shirt, and then stared at her reflection in the mirror. Not much point in trying to compete with Jancis, when it came to looks. Rose combed her mop of gold-brown hair into some kind of order, dabbed on mascara and lip-gloss, and decided that would have to do. It was the way that Nathan always saw her. Either he liked it, or he didn't. And if he didn't, then there wasn't much she could do about it now.

Her feet dragging reluctantly, she finally went downstairs. To her relief, there was no sign of Jancis. She began to make herself a cup of coffee, and then jumped nervously as the kitchen door opened.

It was Nathan. He looked at her steadily for a few moments. Then he came into the kitchen and closed the door behind him. 'Are you angry with me?' he asked in a dry voice.

'Yes, I am,' she said at once. Then she glared at him. 'Why did you *do* it? She's the last person on earth I ever wanted to see!'

Nathan sat down, looking quite relaxed. 'Sometimes, the best way to deal with a problem is to come face to face with it.'

'But bringing her here, to Lyncombe Manor!' Rose banged a couple of mugs down noisily on the table. 'I hate seeing her here. She doesn't belong here.'

'She'd like to,' remarked Nathan.

'I know that.' Rose scowled at him. 'She looks at you as if she'd like to eat you.'

'Which is something of a change,' Nathan said calmly. 'It always used to be the other way round.'

But Rose didn't want to hear about that. 'How did you find her?' she asked, wanting to change the subject.

'It wasn't difficult. I simply rang her agent. He told me where she was staying. He also told me that she had a lot of free time at the moment. Her career's definitely on the slide. Very few bookings, and no new recording contracts.'

Rose supposed she ought to feel sorry for Jancis, but she just couldn't seem to manage it. 'How could her career go downhill so fast?' she said with some curiosity.

Nathan shrugged. 'The public are pretty fickle. You're only as good as your last performance, or your last record. Since we split up, she hasn't been able to find any new material that was good enough to keep her at the top. Her record sales fell off, and her live concerts stopped being a sell-out. Once that starts to happen, the slide downwards becomes very hard to stop.'

'She thought that she didn't need you,' Rose said slowly. 'That she could make it without you. But she can't. So, now she wants you back.'

'Her agent told me that she's been trying to find me,' agreed Nathan. 'No one knew where I had gone, though.'

'Didn't you even tell your friends? Or your family?'

'A couple of close friends knew where to find me. They wouldn't have given my address to Jancis, though. As for family——' he gave an odd little shrug '—I don't have any. I've no idea who my father was, and my mother dumped me at birth. I suppose she had her reasons, but she didn't stick around to explain them. I spent a lot of time in different children's homes, and occasionally I was farmed out to foster parents. None of them kept me for very long, though. Not that I really blame them. I was a pretty difficult child.'

Rose was staring at him in horror by this time. 'That's awful! No one should have that kind of childhood.'

'It wasn't all bad,' he said quickly, seeing the stricken look on her face. 'I remember quite a few good times. And kids in that sort of position tend to stick together. I made some good friends. I still keep in touch with most of them.'

Rose was still thoroughly shaken. She had had such a happy childhood herself that she couldn't bear to think of someone having no close family, no one to turn to in time of trouble, no one who really cared in the way that only loving parents care.

She was too choked up to say anything else for a couple of minutes. Nathan remained silent, as well, as if knowing that she needed a little time to take in what he had told her. Then, when she was finally ready to ask a couple of halting questions, there wasn't a chance because the door opened and Jancis floated in.

When she saw Rose sitting there, her face rapidly altered. The cool blue eyes became hard, and her mouth set into straight lines at the corners.

Rose wasn't in the mood for any sort of confrontation, though. She got to her feet and headed towards the door that led out into the garden. 'I've got a lot of work to get on with,' she said quickly. 'I'll see you later.'

She escaped into the fresh air, and felt a sense of relief once she was out of the house. Lyncombe Manor wasn't the same with Jancis Kendall inside it.

She headed for the far end of the garden. There were several shrubs there that had grown wild and needed clipping back into shape, and at least she would be a safe distance from the house—and Jancis.

While she worked, she couldn't help brooding over what Nathan had told her. No wonder he had fallen into that obsessive relationship with Jancis. He must have been desperately looking for love, after a whole lifetime without it. The bad luck that had dogged him for most of his life had still been following him around, though. He had chosen a woman who didn't seem capable of loving. Only of using and manipulating people.

Rose sighed. And now, Jancis was back again. All right, so Nathan had gone looking for her, and brought her back here, of his own free will. Was he really over her, though? Or was all this just an excuse to get her back into his life again?

She still didn't know the answers. All the old uncertainties kept coming back to plague her. Common sense told her that Nathan must have been sure of his feelings, or he wouldn't have risked coming into contact with her again. Yet common sense flew right out of the window whenever thoughts of Jancis came into Rose's head. Jancis—Nathan's ex-lover. Jancis—who sang his songs so exquisitely. Jancis—who now wanted Nathan, in a way that she had never wanted him before. Although Rose was inexperienced in many ways, she knew that being wanted often ignited a powerful response. And if she, in her relative ignorance, knew that, then it was very certain that Jancis Kendall knew it, too.

Rose hacked away at the shrubs with unnecessary viciousness. She had almost completely decimated a forsythia before realising what she was doing. She dropped the secateurs, and then tiredly rubbed her forehead. This was no good. She had better stop right now, before she did even more damage.

'I'm no gardener, but I don't think that a shrub should be cut right down like that,' commented a cool female voice.

Rose briefly closed her eyes. She really didn't want to see Jancis Kendall right now. 'What are you doing here?' she said flatly.

'I thought that we should have a talk,' replied Jancis. 'We hardly seem to have spoken to each other since I arrived here.'

She moved a little closer, standing in the full sunshine, so that brilliant highlights glinted in her pale hair. She was wearing a white dress in a soft, floating material, and light, strappy sandals.

Rose knew that, in contrast, she looked a mess. Her jeans were faded, her T-shirt was marked with grass stains, and she was sweaty and grubby after attacking that shrub with such unnecessary vigour.

Jancis was looking at her assessingly now, as if trying to figure out what Nathan saw in her. Then she seemed to relax, as if writing her off as no real threat.

'I'm surprised that you want to work in a place like this,' she remarked. 'It must be very dreary, with only Nathan for company.'

'If you think that being with Nathan is dreary, what are *you* doing here?' Rose shot back at once.

Jancis's carefully plucked eyebrows rose gently. 'You want us to be quite honest with each other? No more pretending that we don't really know what's going on? That's fine by me. I prefer it that way.' She flicked back a strand of pale blonde hair that had drifted over her eyes. 'Nathan isn't dreary, of course,' she went on. 'Either in bed, or out. We both know that—or, at least, I assume we do,' she said, looking at Rose assessingly.

Rose managed, with great difficulty, to keep her own face totally expressionless. She *wasn't* going to let this woman provoke her into an angry outburst.

'Of course, I used to pretend that I wasn't interested in him,' Jancis went on. 'That always used to get him going—and Nathan was quite something when he was angry.' Jancis closed her eyes slightly dreamily, as if recalling exactly what it had been like, and Rose shivered convulsively. How much more of this could she take?

'Then I made the mistake of thinking that I could make it without him,' Jancis continued, in a rather different tone. 'I'd made it to the top and I had every-thing—money, fame, best-selling records and adoring fans. I began to ask myself why I needed Nathan any more. He was taking a half-share of everything that came in, and I didn't like that. I was greedy. I wanted it all, so I decided to dump him.'

'According to Nathan, *he* was the one who walked out,' Rose said tightly.

For just a moment, Jancis looked very angry. She obviously liked people only to hear her version of events.

'Whichever way it was, Nathan left,' she said tautly, at last. 'But soon after the split, I realised I'd made a big mistake. I needed Nathan. I wanted him back again. He'd gone, though. It was as if he'd disap-peared off the face of the earth. No one knew where he was, or how to find him.'

'Perhaps that was because he didn't want to be found,' retorted Rose. 'And are you sure it was Nathan you wanted back? Or was it just his songs? You don't seem to have been doing too well since he stopped writing all your material for you.'

Perhaps it was a cruel jibe, but Rose no longer cared. Jancis had caused enough pain—and caused it quite deliberately. Maybe it was her turn to get some of it back again.

Jancis's face didn't look quite so exquisite now. Her blue eyes had narrowed, and her mouth had set into an almost ugly line. 'Yes, I want him to write for me again,' she said in a hard voice. 'And I want our partnership back. I've decided that things are going to be just the way they were.'

'Sometimes, you don't always get what you want,' Rose said steadily.

'I'll get it,' Jancis said with utter confidence. 'I know Nathan. I know what turns him on, what he likes. And this time, I'm going to make sure that he sees a new side of me, the vulnerable side. He'll like that. It's what he's always wanted, to see me vulnerable. He won't be able to resist it.'

Rose turned away from her, and began to pick up the gardening tools she had been using. Then she slowly began to walk away.

'You might as well pack your things and leave right now,' Jancis called after her. 'You'll never have Nathan. I'm the one he's always wanted, and I can get him back again any time I want. You're only second best. Just someone he's turned to because I wasn't around.'

Rose was beginning to feel slightly sick now, but she refused to show any sign of weakness in front of this woman. Ignore her, she told herself steadily. Just keep walking. Get *away* from her, and you'll start to feel better.

But even when Jancis was out of sight, Rose still felt sick to her stomach. Because she was afraid Jancis was right? she asked herself shakily. Jancis had said that she was second best—and that was Rose's own greatest fear. Nathan might like her. He might even want her. But if Jancis still came first, if he still had any of the old feelings for her, then Rose knew that she couldn't bear to live with that.

She stayed out in the garden for most of the rest of the day, only going into the house for a meal when she was sure that neither Nathan nor Jancis were around. She knew how Nathan had spent the day. She had heard the sound of his music drifting out of the open windows of the room where he worked. Was Jancis with him? she wondered with a pang of sheer jealousy. Later in the afternoon, Rose discovered that she wasn't. She had made sure that she stayed very close to him, though, sitting right outside his window, reclining prettily in the shade of a nearby tree, so that he could hardly fail to see her every time he glanced up.

When it finally got too dark to work any longer, Rose reluctantly trudged back into the house. She was tired to the point of exhaustion, every limb aching from the long hours of work she had put in today. Perhaps she was finally tired enough to sleep tonight, she thought hopefully. She felt as if she needed several hours of uninterrupted sleep to stop herself from cracking up.

She had just enough energy left to cook herself a meal. She sat down in the kitchen to eat it, but had only swallowed a couple of mouthfuls when the door opened and Nathan came in.

'Why are you sitting here on your own?' he said, in some surprise. 'Jancis and I are in the drawing-room. Come and join us. Bring your supper with you.'

'I'm the hired help,' Rose muttered. 'And hired help always eat in the kitchen.'

He just looked at her for a few moments. 'Are you being funny?' he said at last.

'Do I look as if I'm laughing?'

He stood there for a while longer. Then he came and sat down opposite her. Rose stopped eating. The last of her meagre appetite seemed to have deserted her.

'You look as if you need a long shower and a good night's sleep,' Nathan said, as his gaze moved over her.

'In other words, I'm a mess!'

Unexpectedly, he reached over and pushed a tousled strand of hair out of her eyes. The gesture unsettled her. Worse than that, it made her eyes prickle. She blinked very hard a couple of times. This wouldn't be a good time to cry.

'Did I make a bad mistake, bringing Jancis here?'

She hadn't been expecting him to say anything like that, and she didn't know how to answer him.

'I thought it might solve the problem we were having,' went on Nathan. 'I didn't mean to make things worse.'

'I don't see how it could have solved anything,' she muttered.

'The best way to lay a ghost is to come face to face with it,' he told her. 'I don't want us to spend the rest of our lives being haunted by Jancis.'

'Are you sure that you didn't just want to see her again?' she shot back immediately.

Nathan withdrew his hand, and the expression on his face began to change. 'We've been through all this before,' he said in a much tighter tone. 'I don't think I can go through it all again.'

'I don't see why not,' Rose said stonily. '*I* didn't want to meet Jancis. *I* didn't want to know anything about her. Yet here she is, back in your life again.

And how did she get here? You went and fetched her back!'

He glared back at her stormily. 'And I've explained why I brought her here! If you can't understand my reasons, then perhaps things aren't as good between us as I thought they were.'

Rose got to her feet and began to move towards the door. 'I think I'm beginning to understand only too well.'

'Where are you going?' he demanded sharply.

'Up to my room. Spending the evening with you and Jancis is just a little more than I can stomach!'

'You haven't eaten your supper.'

'Give it to her!' she flung back at him, as she wrenched open the door. 'She seems to want everything else that I thought was mine. Why shouldn't she have my food as well?'

She charged out of the kitchen after that, slamming the door behind her with a very satisfying thud. She knew she was behaving rather childishly, but she didn't care. Losing her temper like that had made her feel much better, and for the first time today that faint sensation of nausea had gone.

Rose went straight up to the east wing, and the privacy of her own rooms. She spent a long time bathing, and washing her hair. Then she sat and slowly brushed the gold-brown curls until they were dry.

She had thought—hoped?—that Nathan might come after her, but there hadn't been any sound of footsteps outside the door. He's probably having such a good time with Jancis that he's forgotten all about me, she told herself with a dark scowl. One thing was absolutely certain. Jancis would make good use of every moment she was left alone with Nathan. Was

she putting on her vulnerable act already? Telling
Nathan that she needed him, that she really loved him,
that she just couldn't make it without him? And was
he falling for it?

Rose put down the brush with some force, not
caring that she had actually made a small dent in the
top of the dresser.

'Men are so gullible,' she muttered to herself.
'Especially where women are concerned. He's
probably swallowing every lie that she's feeding him.'

She pulled on her cotton nightshirt, but knew that
she wasn't ready to go to bed yet. The tiredness that
had swept over her earlier seemed to have disappeared and, on top of that, she was hungry. If she
had had any sense, she would have finished her supper
before she began that scene with Nathan.

She decided to go down to the kitchen, and make
herself a sandwich. First of all, though, she wanted
to make very sure that there was no chance of bumping
into either Nathan or Jancis.

The east wing had been built on to the back of the
house at right angles, so she could see the windows
in the main part of the house from here. No lights
showed anywhere, which must mean that the other
two had gone to bed. Rose refused to consider the
possibility that they might have gone together. She
had already gone through enough today. She wasn't
deliberately going to add to her own misery.

Silently, she made her way through the darkened
house. She knew her way around well enough by now,
and didn't switch on any lights until she reached the
kitchen.

It didn't take her long to make a sandwich. She
decided to take it back to her room and eat it there,

rather than in the kitchen. That way, she could at least be sure no one would coming barging in and ruin her appetite for a second time!

She slipped back up the stairs, and was just about to go through the doorway that led to the east wing when she thought she heard a creaking sound on the stairs behind her.

'Is someone there?' she called out in a soft but quavering voice.

'Of course there is,' replied Nathan's voice from the darkness. 'Who did you think it was? The Lyncombe ghost?'

A couple of seconds later, he was standing beside her, although she could only just see him in the shadows at the top of the stairs. Rose moved a little restlessly. Lately, being this close to him was never easy.

'Mind that you don't drop your sandwich,' he warned, a hint of amusement lightening his tone now.

'How do you know that I've got a sandwich?' she demanded. 'Have you been watching me?'

'Not exactly. I was sitting in the great hall, and I heard you come down to the kitchen. I guessed you were making yourself a snack.'

'I didn't see any lights on in the hall.'

'That's because I'd turned them off,' Nathan replied equably.

'Why?'

'I had some thinking to do. And it's often easier to think more clearly when you're sitting alone in the dark.'

Well, at least he had been alone, Rose told herself with a rush of relief. She could forget about those tormenting pictures of him and Jancis together. 'Why did you follow me up here?' she asked, after a short pause.

'I'd have thought that was fairly obvious,' Nathan said a little huskily. 'I'm tired of my own company. I want someone to share the rest of the night with. To be more precise, I want you.'

'No,' Rose said instinctively.

She heard his sharp intake of breath. 'That sounded very definite,' he said at length, his tone no longer so relaxed.

'I didn't mean to be quite so blunt,' she said in a low voice. 'But I did mean it,' she added quickly, as he began to move closer in the darkness.

His fingers lightly ran up the length of her spine, and she shivered involuntarily in response. 'Are you sure of that?' he asked softly.

Rose couldn't answer for a moment. Her throat seemed to have become too tight.

His fingers danced a little higher, finding the vulnerable skin at the nape of her neck. At the same time, she heard his breathing begin to change. He was already reacting to her closeness, and she sensed the stirring of his body as he leant towards her, searching for the warmth of her mouth.

Rose knew that if she let him kiss her, then she would be lost. At the last moment, she turned her head away. She heard his frustrated mutter; then he moved nearer again, trying to force her into closer contact with him.

'Don't!' she said, almost pleadingly.

'Why not?' he growled.

'Because I don't want to. Not while *she's* in this house!'

Her blurted answer seemed to startle him. Nathan let go of her, took a step back, and then stared down at her intently in the darkness.

'Are you sure that's the only reason?'

'Of course it is!'

He seemed to begin to relax again. 'Then perhaps I'd better do something about the situation,' he said, the dry amusement beginning to return to his voice again. 'I don't think I can go on like this for very much longer!' He gave her a gentle push. 'Go on back to your room, Rose. Eat your sandwich, sleep well, and we'll try and sort everything out in the morning.'

Her feet dragging, Rose turned away from him and trailed back to her room. She closed the door behind her, and threw her sandwich to one side. She was no longer hungry—at least, not for food.

She had realised by now that she hadn't actually wanted him to go. So why did you send him away? she asked with a deep sigh.

Because she had told him the truth, she answered herself a moment later. The spectre of Jancis still hung over this house. And no amount of lovemaking would ever quite exorcise it.

She crawled into bed and tried to sleep, but it was impossible. A clock in the distance chimed midnight, and Rose got up and walked over to the window. It felt stifling in the bedroom. She opened the window wider, to let in some fresh air, and then froze as she heard a door open below.

A moment later, the sound of Jancis's voice drifted up to her.

'Come on, Nathan. It'll be fun. Remember the last time we swam at midnight? It was on the Riviera, at the end of that European tour. I remember how it

ended, as well——' She gave a low, throaty laugh, and
Rose's skin actually crawled. She hated this woman.
It was the first time in her life that she had felt such
a strong loathing for another human being. She didn't
like feeling this way, but she just couldn't help it.

Surely Nathan wasn't going to go with her, though?
Rose hid behind the net curtain, and waited for him
to tell Jancis that if she wanted to go swimming at
midnight she would have to go alone.

Instead, though, she saw him walking along the
path beside her. She could hardly believe it, but that
tall, lean figure was quite unmistakable, even in the
insipid light from the waning moon overhead.

Rose closed her eyes. She didn't want to see this!
Then she slowly opened them again. Perhaps it was
time to find out exactly what was going on, she told
herself, fighting back the faint sensation of sickness
that had returned to her stomach. Nathan had told
her just a short while ago that he was going to sort
everything out in the morning. Well, perhaps she
wasn't going to like the changes that he clearly intended to make.

Acting on pure instinct now, Rose slid her feet into
a pair of soft-soled sandals. She didn't bother to dress.
Instead, still wearing just her nightshirt, she ran lightly
down through the house and then out into the garden.

Nathan and Jancis had disappeared from sight by
now, but she was certain that she knew where they
were going. The cove at the end of the valley. The
cove where Nathan had told her that she had beautiful
breasts . . .

She forced herself not to think of it. A special kind
of madness lay that way. Instead, she walked steadily

along the path, her feet not stumbling once in the darkness.

The night was warm and sweet-scented, but it could have been blowing a blizzard for all Rose knew or cared. She walked blindly on, dreading what she might see, but quite incapable of turning back.

When she finally reached the cove, she found that Nathan and Jancis were already on the beach. The sea rippled softly on to the sand, and the water glinted with silver lights as it reflected the pale glow of the moon.

Rose stayed in the shadows of the rocks at the back of the cove. She knew that she couldn't be seen, and she had a perfect view of the beach as it sloped gently down to the sea.

Jancis was beginning to strip off her clothes now. With a total lack of inhibition, her white dress was discarded, and her lace petticoat. And it soon became clear that she didn't intend to stop there. Her bra and panties were quickly tossed aside, and then she stood naked in the moonlight.

Her body was as perfect as her face. Full, high breasts, a narrow waist and slim hips. Rose almost groaned out loud. How could she possibly ever compete with that? she thought in sheer misery.

All the same, she realised that she had hoped all along that Nathan would stop, would turn back, before things began to go too far. That hope finally began to slide away from her as she saw him begin to strip off his own clothes. Rose's gaze slid over him, and she shivered convulsively. She remembered how that firm, hard body had felt as it had moved against hers. She remembered too many things—things that were going to be hard—quite impossible—to forget.

Jancis was in the water now, and Nathan walked down to join her. He was a strong swimmer, and he swam some distance out to sea, while Jancis languidly played around in the shallower water.

Rose knew that she ought to go now. She had seen more than enough. Something kept her rooted to the spot, though—some perverse force that seemed determined to make her see even more.

They finally left the water, and Rose prayed softly that all her suspicions would be proved wrong. Perhaps they *had* just come down for a quite innocent swim. All right, so she would have felt a lot better if they had worn swimsuits. There wasn't anything so very terrible about nakedness, though. After all, they were old friends.

No, not old friends. Old lovers, she silently corrected herself, a moment later. And, somehow, that made all the difference in the world.

They had returned to the spot where they had left their clothes, and Rose waited in anguish, willing them to put them back on. Instead, though, she felt her heart actually stop beating for a few seconds as Jancis slowly reached out and placed her hand on Nathan's wet body.

Turn round and walk away from her! she pleaded with him silently. Do it *now*.

But Nathan didn't move. Nor did he try to pull away when Jancis moved closer, her hands touching more intimately, and her face raised to his, searching for his mouth.

Rose couldn't watch for one more second. A choked sound came from her throat; then she turned her back on them, and bolted.

She didn't remember anything of her frantic rush
back to the house. Only of arriving back in her room,
shaking and gasping for breath. She tore off her
nightshirt, somehow fumbled her way into jeans and
a sweatshirt, and then began frantically opening cupboards and drawers, dragging out her possessions.

As she hurled them into her suitcases, she told
herself that there was no need to rush like this. Nathan
was going to be fully occupied for some time yet.

She didn't want to stay in this house for one second
longer than she had to, though. All the same, she had
to sit on the edge of the bed for a few minutes, to try
and steady her shaking body. She was going to have
to drive her car in a moment, and right now she was
in no fit state. With a huge effort, she managed to
get some control over her trembling limbs. Then she
picked up her suitcases, and stumbled downstairs.

More time was lost, because she couldn't find her
car keys. Panic-stricken, she fumbled around in her
suitcases for what seemed like ages. She had to be out
of here before they got back!

She finally found them in her bag, caught behind
a tear in the lining. With a sigh of relief, she rushed
out to the car, threw her suitcases in the back and
flopped into the driving seat.

The engine started first time, and the car shot off
down the drive. And as Lyncombe Manor disappeared behind her into the darkness, Rose wondered
if Nathan would know—if he would *ever* know—what
it was costing her to run out on him like this.

CHAPTER NINE

THE lane leading away from Lyncombe Manor was completely unlit. Rose knew that she was driving far too fast, but she still kept her foot pressed down hard on the accelerator. The car skidded round the dark bends, and she just prayed that she wouldn't meet anything coming in the other direction.

She couldn't even see properly now, because her eyes were blurred with tears. She rubbed them away with the back of her hand, but more came to take their place.

A straight stretch of road lay ahead of her, and the car rattled along even faster. There was a sharp bend at the end, though, and Rose suddenly realised that she had misjudged it; she wasn't going to make it.

She stamped frantically on the brakes, and the car swung wildly from side to side. Then it settled into a long skid. Rose tried to steer into it, but it was too late to correct it. She finally ran out of road, and there was nothing she could do except brace herself against the inevitable impact.

The car ran up the bank at the side of the road, and then jolted to an abrupt halt as it plunged into the shallow ditch on the other side. The engine died, and there was an eerie silence after all the noise and confusion.

Rose was bruised and thoroughly shaken, but she gradually realised that she wasn't badly hurt. Although she had rushed away from Lyncombe Manor in a frantic hurry, she had still automatically clicked on the seatbelt when she had got into the car. That simple reflex action had saved her from serious injury.

It was a long time before she could do anything except sit there and tremble, though. On top of everything else that had happened tonight, it was just too much to cope with.

Finally, she eased her aching body into a more comfortable position. Then, with fingers that were still very unsteady, she switched on the ignition.

The car started, but that was all. It had obviously suffered major damage when it had plunged over that bank and into the ditch, and it wouldn't move.

Rose stared blindly into the darkness. What was she going to do now? Go back to Lyncombe Manor and phone a local garage, to see if they could get her back on the road?

No, she decided immediately, with a small shudder. She was never going to set foot in that house again!

Which didn't leave her much alternative, except to start walking in the other direction. She tried to figure out how far she had come, and knew it wasn't any distance at all. She would have a walk of a couple of miles, perhaps even further, along this pitch-dark lane before she reached the nearest house. And right now she didn't feel up to walking even a few yards.

She sat there in the car for a few more minutes, because it was all she could seem to do. The effort required to get out and start walking was just totally beyond her. Her shoulders slumped and she could feel the tears burning at the back of her eyes again as the full shock of everything that had happened began to roll over her.

Then, even through her growing misery, she began to realise that she could see lights glowing in the road behind. Another car? she thought, with a small spurt of hope. Someone who would stop and help her?

It was a car, and to her relief it stopped. Rose could hardly believe that something was finally going to go right. Then she got a good look at the tall figure who had got out and was racing towards her, and her eyes flew wide open. Oh, no, she gulped. It *couldn't* be!

Nathan wrenched open the door and slid into the seat beside her. 'What the hell happened? Are you hurt? Damn!' he muttered under his breath. 'It's too dark in here. I can't see you.'

He switched on the interior light of the car which, miraculously, was still working. Rose could see now that his face looked as pale and shocked as her own must be. He began to run his hands over her, searching for any sign of injury.

Rose flinched and instinctively drew back. 'Don't,' she muttered. 'I'm all right.'

'If you're all right, what are you doing sitting in a wrecked car in the middle of the night?' he said tautly.

'I wanted to get away,' she said in a voice that was still horribly shaky. 'Only, the car ran off the road.'

'Who were you trying to get away from?' he demanded grimly. 'Me?'

'Yes, from you!' she flung back at him, in a sudden burst of defiance.

He sat back in the seat, no longer trying to touch her. 'You saw what happened tonight, didn't you?' he said flatly, at last. 'On the beach, I mean.'

But Rose didn't want to talk about that. She didn't even want to *think* about it.

'I know that you followed us down to the cove to-night,' he went on, in the same level tone. 'On my way back to the house, I found your sandal on the path.'

Rose didn't remember losing a sandal. That wasn't surprising, though. She didn't remember anything about that headlong flight back to Lyncombe Manor.

'How much did you see?' he asked her, looking straight at her now with disconcerting intensity.

'Enough,' she muttered.

'I don't think so.'

At that, she lifted her head and glared at him. 'I saw you both naked! I saw her touching you! I saw her beginning to kiss you! How much more did you want me to see?'

Nathan's eyes glittered. 'If you'd stayed a few more minutes, you'd have seen that it went no further than that.'

She threw a look of sheer contempt at him. 'Do you really expect me to believe that? I might be a bit of an innocent—at least, compared with *her*—but I'm not totally gullible.'

Nathan swore softly under his breath. Then he seized hold of her shoulders and forcibly twisted her round, so that she was directly facing him. 'Think again about what you saw!' he ordered. 'All right, so I was naked. But was I aroused? Did I look as if I wanted her?'

Rose felt herself flushing. 'No, you didn't,' she muttered. 'But you let her touch you,' she added, with a fresh flare of misery. 'You let her kiss you.'

'And did I do either of those things back to her?' demanded Nathan.

'No,' she said again, after a very long pause.

'Doesn't that tell you something?'

But Rose wasn't ready to listen to reason yet. 'Why did you go to the beach with her, in the first place?' she challenged him fiercely. 'Why did you let her get so close to you?'

This time, it was Nathan who hesitated before replying. 'Perhaps I needed to prove something to myself,' he said at last.

'And you had to run around naked with her, to do that?' she said scornfully.

'It seemed as good a way as any to make absolutely sure that I really didn't want her any more.'

It took her a couple of minutes to digest that remark, and consider all its implications. 'You kept telling me that you *were* sure,' she said finally, her tone still hostile.

'I was ninety-nine per cent sure. When you've been that deeply involved with someone, though, there's always the small fear that it might not be quite over. That there still might be some way they could get to you. That's why I stayed away from Jancis for such a long time. Part of me was always a little afraid of coming face to face with her again.'

Rose remembered him telling her that they both had problems that needed solving. She was beginning to understand now what he had meant by that.

'And what if she *had* still been able to get to you?' she asked, her voice more subdued now.

'I'd have told you,' he said at once. 'And, together, we would have had to decide whether we could cope with that extra complication. The question doesn't arise, though. She *doesn't* get to me. I proved that tonight, in the most positive way possible.'

Rose slowly began to believe what he was telling her. And with that belief came a sense of relief that was so strong that it almost overwhelmed her. 'I don't suppose Jancis was very pleased when she found she wasn't getting any response from you,' she said, almost cheerfully.

'No, she wasn't,' agreed Nathan drily.

'She really did want you, you know.'

'Yes, she finally did want me. But I don't think she'd have been so determined to get me if she hadn't thought that she'd also be getting some new material for her act at the same time. Jancis wants to be a star again. She wants to get back all the very pleasant trappings of success—the money, the adulation, the endless publicity. She thought I was the man who could make it happen for her.'

Rose could imagine how Jancis had reacted when she'd found that none of it was going to work out as she had planned. 'Is she back at the house?' she asked, unable to suppress a small shiver at the thought of having to see her again.

Nathan noted the shiver, and immediately put his arm around her. 'She should have left by now,' he told her. 'Jancis took it rather badly when her plan to seduce me didn't work out. There was quite a scene when we finally got back to the house. She showed the true side of her character for once—and it wasn't very pleasant,' he added, with a grimace. 'I'd had more than enough of her, by then. I realised that bringing her here in the first place hadn't been one of my better ideas. I'd thought it would help to solve the problems we'd been having, but instead it had simply driven you away. I told Jancis to phone for a taxi, and get out straight away.'

'At one o'clock in the morning?' said Rose, with raised eyebrows.

'I didn't care what time it was. I wanted her away from the house, and out of my life. You probably didn't notice, but a car passed us several minutes ago. Jancis should have been in it.'

Rose looked at him a little uncertainly. 'What should we do now, then?' she asked in a low voice.

'I think we should go home.'

Home—Rose savoured the word. And Lyncombe Manor *did* seem like home. At least, it would now that Jancis was no longer there.

Nathan helped her out of the wreck of her car, and kept his arm firmly round her waist as he guided her over to his own car, which was just a few yards away. She sank into the front seat, gave a small sigh of tired relief, and never took her eyes from the pale outline of his face as he drove them back to Lyncombe Manor.

As they got out of the car and walked slowly towards the front entrance, her heart began to thump a lot faster than usual. And because his hand was tightly wrapped around her own, she could feel the answering beat of his own pulse.

Once they were inside the house, Nathan turned to her. 'Now that we've finally laid the ghost of Jancis, how do you suppose we should spend the rest of the night?' he said softly. Before Rose had a chance to answer, though, he suddenly lifted his head. 'Do you smell something?' he asked, much more sharply.

Now that he had drawn her attention to it, Rose could. An acrid smell, that seemed to be steadily getting stronger.

Nathan's face abruptly went very white, while his slate-grey eyes blazed with pure anger. 'The bitch!'

he said in a savage tone. 'She warned me that she'd make me pay, and she has. She's set fire to the house!'

He was moving even as he spoke, breaking into a run. Rose blinked in dazed disbelief for a few moments. Then she gathered her wits together and ran after him.

Nathan swiftly made his way along the corridor that led to the east wing. At the far end, he came to an abrupt halt. There was no need to look any further for the source of the fire. Smoke was visibly seeping from under one of the closed doors, creating a steadily thickening fog in the corridor.

He seized hold of Rose. 'There's a fire extinguisher in the great hall,' he said rapidly. 'I'll use it to try and contain the fire. Go and ring for the fire brigade. Then get the extinguisher in the kitchen, and bring it here as quickly as you can.'

'Be careful,' begged Rose.

He gave her a none too gentle push. 'Get to the phone—now!'

She didn't need to be told again. She rushed to the nearest extension and, with trembling fingers, phoned the emergency number. To her relief, they answered almost at once. She gabbled the replies to the quick questions they asked her. Then, once she was sure they were on their way, she dashed to the kitchen to fetch the other extinguisher.

It was too heavy for her to carry. Gasping for breath, she dragged it along to the corridor to where Nathan was already tackling the blaze.

The door where the smoke had been seeping out was open now, and the room beyond seemed to be filled with heat and flames. Rose stared at in horror. How could they possibly hope to do anything about it? It would be like throwing a bucket of water on to a forest fire!

The fire extinguisher was empty now, and Nathan tossed it to one side. As he took the second one from Rose, he spoke to her very rapidly. 'It looks worse than it is. It's already beginning to get a good hold, though. If we let it get away from us, then the whole house could go up.'

'What can we do?' she asked in a frightened voice.

'I want to get some of that combustible material out of there.'

'You'll be burnt to death!'

'No, I won't,' he said firmly. 'I'll toss what I can out to you. Make sure none of it's smouldering. We don't want to start another fire in the corridor!'

Using the second fire extinguisher to keep the area around him free from flames, he advanced slowly into the room. Rose could hardly bear to watch. She wouldn't be able to stand it if anything happened to him.

Nathan pulled down the heavy curtains and threw them over to her. They were already beginning to smoulder around the edges, and Rose hastily stamped on them until the small flames were extinguished. Next, he threw out cushions, magazines, a couple of small wooden tables, anything that would help to feed the fire.

It was a battle that he couldn't hope to win, though. The flames slowly began to advance on him, and Rose's blood ran cold as she realised that he was almost surrounded now by those bright, flickering tongues.

'Get out of there!' she yelled at him in sudden panic. And when he didn't seem to hear her, she dashed into the room, grabbed hold of his shirt and physically dragged him towards the door.

Only seconds later, a sheet of flame flashed right across the spot where he had been standing. Nathan stared at it blankly for a few seconds, as if slowly realising just how much danger he had been in. Then he seemed to pull himself together again, and quickly turned towards her.

'Is there a hose in that shed where all the garden equipment's kept?' he asked, coughing now as the smoke began to get down his lungs.

Rose tried to remember if she had seen one. 'I think so,' she said at last.

'Go and take a look. If you find it, fix it to the tap in the kitchen. And hurry!'

She hated to leave him. She was afraid of what he might do to try and save this house. The second extinguisher must be almost empty, and they didn't know how much longer it would be until the fire brigade arrived.

Rose tore through the house and out across the courtyard. When she finally reached the shed, she was dismayed to find it in total darkness. Why hadn't she thought to bring a torch? No time to go back and fetch one, she told herself shakily. Just find that hose!

She scrambled among the lawnmowers, spades, rakes and shears, cracked her ankle on the wheelbarrow, and tripped over a broom. Her eyes had adjusted slightly to the lack of light, but it was still difficult to see anything clearly. In the end, she simply groped around, praying that her grubby, bruised fingers would finally find something that felt like a hose.

More by luck than anything else, she found it only seconds later. Then she almost wept in frustration, because it was a long hose, and too heavy for her to carry more than a short distance.

Just in time, she remembered the wheelbarrow. Frantically, she began to pile the coils in. Then she staggered back to the house, her lungs wheezing and gasping by the time she had finally pushed that heavy weight as far as the kitchen.

To her relief, Nathan came through the door only seconds later. Between the two of them, they managed to get the hose hooked up to the tap in a remarkably short time. Then Nathan swiftly began to haul its length through the house, to the source of the fire.

Rose stayed in the kitchen, to turn on the tap at his shouted command. And when she finally rejoined him, she was alarmed to see how much fiercer the fire had become.

The water that gushed out of the hose seemed to have frighteningly little effect. As fast as the flames were doused in one area, they sprang up in another.

Nathan suddenly seemed to realise that she was standing beside him. 'I want you to get out of here,' he told her in a grim voice. 'Right out of the house, Rose. It's too dangerous for you to stay here any longer.'

'I'm not going until you do,' she said stubbornly.

'It isn't safe!'

'I don't care. I'm not going to leave you!'

He looked as if he was going to argue fiercely with her. Instead, though, to her complete astonishment, he suddenly turned and gave her a swift, hard kiss.

At almost the same time, above the crackle and roar of the flames, Rose heard the sound of the fire brigade arriving.

It seemed only seconds later that everything was taken out of their hands. They were shunted unceremoniously outside, leaving the fire in the capable hands of the professionals. The firemen doused it in a remarkably short time. Then they began a thorough search of the house, to make sure that nothing had been left to smoulder and perhaps flare up again later.

A couple of hours later, it was at last all over. Rose could hardly believe that this long night was finally coming to an end, that they were both safe and uninjured, and that the main part of the house had escaped with very little damage.

One of the firemen had already lectured them on the dangers of trying to fight a fire without the proper equipment. Then he had relaxed a little, and told them that their efforts had probably saved the house from extensive damage. As it was, the room where the fire had started and a couple of rooms above it had suffered quite severely. There had also been quite a lot of smoke damage in the east wing. Everything could be restored in time, though, and Rose knew they were very lucky that the entire house hadn't gone up in flames.

The fireman had also wanted her and Nathan to go to the hospital, for a routine check-up. They had both refused. All they had wanted by that time was to be left alone, at Lyncombe Manor.

The last of the fire engines finally rolled away, and an air of peace began to return to the house. Nathan and Rose made their way to the great hall, which had been completely untouched by the fire. Then they just stood and looked at each other for a couple of minutes.

'You saved my life,' Nathan said at last. 'If you hadn't pulled me out of that room, I'd have been burned to a cinder by that sheet of flame.'

Rose shivered as she remembered how the fire had suddenly swept across the very spot where he had been standing. 'I don't want to think about it,' she said in an unsteady voice. 'Not right now.' She looked at him. 'What will happen to Jancis?'

'Nothing, I should think,' Nathan said in a hard tone. 'We both know that she started that fire, but it would be almost impossible to prove it in a court of law.'

'Then she'll get away with it?'

'With the fire—yes.'

'Do you think that it was just a coincidence that it started in the east wing?' asked Rose, with another shiver. 'The wing where I was staying?'

'Of course not. Jancis has a very vindictive streak. And it certainly showed itself tonight.' The line of Nathan's mouth tightened. 'But there are ways to make her pay for what she did.'

Rose looked at him. 'How?'

'I still have a lot of influential contacts in the music business. That particular lady is going to find it very hard to pursue her career, from now on. She'll find that promoters won't want to book her, none of the top agents will want to take her on, and record companies will be even less enthusiastic to offer her a new recording contract than they are right now. Up until now, her career's been on a gentle downhill slide,' he said grimly. 'From now on, it's going to take a spectacular plunge.'

She bit her lip. 'Is it fair to do that to her?' she said at last.

Nathan stared at her incredulously. 'After tonight, how can you say that? One—or even both—of us could easily have been killed. She started that fire quite deliberately. She wanted to destroy this house, and she didn't particularly care if she also destroyed us in the process.'

'I think——' Rose hesitated, and then began again. 'I think that losing you—and losing your songs—is probably punishment enough.'

'You're too soft,' he said, with a shake of his head. Then his mouth slowly began to relax into the faintest shadow of a smile. 'But that's probably one of the things that makes me want to stay with you. And if that's what you really want——'

'Yes, it is. I hate her,' she confessed, 'but I don't want to be like her in any way. To ruin a career that's already almost over—that would mean we'd be behaving just as vindictively as she did.'

Nathan shrugged in resigned acceptance. 'Then I won't make any of those phone calls. And we'll try not to mention her name again for the rest of our lives.'

The rest of their lives—that sounded to Rose as if he had some fairly far-reaching plans for their future. And after tonight, she was finally willing to believe that that future did exist.

'Are you telling me that you want me to stay here with you, at Lyncombe Manor?' she asked a little shyly.

'As a matter of fact, I intend to give you the house as a wedding present,' he said casually. 'Of course, it's a rather damaged present, at the moment. It shouldn't take more than a few weeks to put right, though.'

Rose stared at him in wide-eyed astonishment. 'Did you say—a wedding present?' she blurted out, at last.

'You're the kind of girl who needs security,' he told her. 'And I want to give you that security.'

'But—you haven't even told me that you—well, that you love me,' she stuttered.

'No, I haven't,' he agreed. 'But I expect I'll eventually get round to it.'

'I didn't know—that is, I never expected—I didn't know you thought of me in that way,' she finally managed to get out.

'In what way?' Nathan enquired, his tone lightly teasing now.

'Well—as something permanent in your life.'

Now it was his turn to look surprised. 'I thought you understood how I felt about you? All right, so we went through all that nonsense over Jancis, but you must have known that I'd decided that you were the one I wanted?'

'I was never really sure,' Rose admitted. 'I still kept feeling as if I were only second best. I know it was silly, but I just couldn't help it. I suppose the real trouble was that I wanted you to feel about me the same way you felt about her.'

'But that's exactly what I *didn't* want,' Nathan said firmly. 'I don't want to feel like that ever again in my entire life. It was a temporary madness. All I want from now on is what we've found together. Something that we can build on. Something that's very solid and real and lasting.'

'Put like that, it also sounds a little dull,' she said with a wry grimace.

Nathan seized hold of her, pulled her very close, and kissed her extremely thoroughly. By the time he had finished, they were both breathing rather erratically, and Rose felt slightly dizzy.

'Did that feel dull?' he demanded.

Rose shook her head, not quite sure she could say anything coherent yet.

'Did that night we spent in bed together seem dull?' he questioned her fiercely.

'No,' she said at once, managing to find her voice again.

'Good,' he said, with some satisfaction. Then he gave a crooked smile. 'I've been accused of quite a few things in my time, but never of being dull!'

'Oh, you're not!' said Rose, with some feeling. 'Life has been full of surprises ever since I first bumped into you, and you locked me in the cellar!'

'And I dare say there are a few more surprises still to come,' he warned her, his eyes glinting. Then his face became more serious. 'But just so we can get this straight once and for all, I want you to know a couple of things. I wanted Jancis. It was a purely physical desire, though. I showed you how that felt,' he reminded her, 'and you didn't like it. I didn't like it, either, but for a long time I couldn't seem to do anything about it. I don't know why. I suppose men have less control over their sex drives than women. I don't want her any more, though, and I'm never going to want her again. But I do want you. More than that, though, I need you. And I love you. I don't know how it happened, and I don't think I particularly want to know. I just thank God that you came crashing into my life and then decided to stick around. Now, do you want to marry me, or not?'

'Yes,' she said at once, without even thinking about it.

'Good,' he said, with some satisfaction. Then he looked at her, and grinned. 'You're filthy.'

'So are you,' she retorted, rubbing with her hand at a sooty smudge on his face.

Nathan turned his head and kissed her fingers. Then he lightly bit them.

'I think we'll take a bath—together,' he said thoughtfully. 'Then we'll have a long sleep—together. And when we wake up...'

'Yes?' she said a little breathlessly, as he stopped nibbling at her fingers and instead lightly stroked the small curve of her breast.

'Then we'll think of some very interesting ways to pass the rest of the day,' he told her huskily.

And that sounded to Rose like the perfect way to spend the next twenty-four hours. In fact, it seemed that the rest of her life was going to turn out to be unexpectedly perfect.

A ROMANTIC TREAT FOR YOU AND YOUR FRIENDS THIS CHRISTMAS

Four exciting new romances, first time in paperback, by some of your favourite authors – delightfully presented as a special gift for Christmas.

THE COLOUR OF DESIRE
Emma Darcy

CONSENTING ADULTS
Sandra Marton

INTIMATE DECEPTION
Kay Thorpe

DESERT HOSTAGE
Sara Wood

For only £5.80 treat yourself to four heartwarming stories.

Look out for the special pack from 12th October, 1990.